Harry's Fr

Harry's Fragments

a novel of international puzzlement

George Bowering

Coach House Press · Toronto

Punctuation adheres carefully to the
author's instructions.

Canadian Cataloguing in Publication Data

Bowering, George, 1935-
Harry's fragments

I. Title.

ISBN 0-88910-397-9

PS8503.092H37 1990   C813'.54   C90-094784-5
PR9199.3.B69H37 1990

for Mike Ondaatje in flux

1 · Way to Go

He thought he would not be able to understand anything in Sydney.

The first day here, anyway. It was summer instead of winter, after all. The sun would be in the north, after all. It was earlier by the clock but later by the calendar, and hours had rolled up under his eyelids. He thought he would not understand even after he saw it.

But the city and the harbour were lying under an ocean-wide sea of cloud. The local is eternal, too. The sun was dispersed into shadowless light. In the Thai restaurant on Oxford Street, the prawn and chili soup tasted like the prawn and chili soup in Toronto and Seattle.

He had seen the woman in a Thai restaurant on Bloor Street West in Toronto. He had been spoken to by her in a Thai restaurant on South Washington Street in Seattle.

The local is eternal, but men and women are unable to understand it. Most men and women. In Seattle he had sat at his formica table and looked at her as she stepped out of the measly restaurant into the rain. He looked at her, and for a moment he was not sure she was a woman.

At the Sydney airport he watched the stunned Americans getting into line. They seemed incapable of knowing the local, though that was their eager purpose. They were asleep.

In line he listened to three Americans talking about the world, and they could have been in Ohio. He was looking around for signs. The signs were in English words, eternal and everywhere, but not equal everywhere.

On the street at last he found the sign he was looking for. Standing on his sore feet in loafers that were too big, but they were the second pair in a two-for-one sale. Four-for-two. The sign was just what she or he had said. Quality Funerals. We Invite Comparisons. White words on mauve walls.

It was a singular message. We must, he said to no one but the wino lying on the sidewalk beside his marvellously standing bottle, consider each thing according to its nature.

The wino was asleep. He was from the Antipodes, a local, but he did not understand anything.

· 2 ·

The next day there was a blue sky, and Oxford Street was filled with people carrying plastic bags with words on them.

The Pacific wind blew skirts against legs. There was a roar in the sky as the British Concorde lifted off and headed for home. There was a hoot in the harbour, as an outbound cruise ship saluted the Queen Elizabeth 2, moored at the Circular Quay. The Concorde, the QE2 and he had arrived in Sydney yesterday, St. Valentine's Day. Human ingenuity had concurred to make such things possible. The local is understandable to all people, or none would be here.

Yet he thought he was here with a secret, or rather part of a secret, not enough. Still enough to have brought him all these thousands of kilometers of air as surely as Qantas had.

What she had said to him before she left the measly restaurant in Seattle would not have been enough to do that. But he had seen her in the melting snow in Kitsilano, waving her hand. He was for the moment a taxi driver. He stopped, but she only waved her hand some more, enough to drop the words on paper in through his window. He looked down to find them on the floor. When he looked up again she was gone. The words were enough to bring him to Sydney. Where else in the world?

Was he foolish to think that there was no one else who knew about this? Knew more than he did? Someone must, if simply because he knew so little.

He walked half a block up from Oxford Street, and saw the two signs hanging over the sidewalk. The first said Quality Funerals. The bottom of the second sign said Killed on the Premises. But when he got closer the signs separated and he saw that the second was in reference to poultry.

· 3 ·

I did not come half way around the world I love to turn away when knowledge makes itself available, he said secretly to his body, because the latter was edging away from the door.

Understanding was what he had wanted since seeing the woman for the second time, and he had known this even more when she had spoken to him. Details later, the end of her remark seemed to say, and so far it was true. Not enough of them, though, or rather, he would have preferred to have more. Well, he was here in New South Wales.

A great many details, please. One for each kilometer in the sky.

He opened the door, and there was no suggestive chime, no electric sound at all, and went in. Inside it was cool enough for corpses.

What could he possible say to the person, likely a man, whose footsteps he heard approaching?

—Yes, said the little man with the big horn-rimmed

9

glasses, you are here as we were advised you would be, but perhaps yesterday.

– Here?

– Yes, follow me, please.

The little man led him further into the cool air and more artificial light. Led him to a casket on a low support, made no gesture with his hand, but stepped backward into comparative darkness.

He looked into the casket, as what else could he do, having followed the advice thus far, quality.

It was, likely, she. Till now his memory had been principally of gesture and movement, toward, briefly, and away. Now he had time, with discomfort fading, to look with his eyes at home now in the yellowish light. He saw that it was nearly certainly she, and now he had time to take in a great number of details. One was a white cloth wrapped around her neck. It was probably shot silk, probably from Taipei.

He took in details for half an hour, probably, but he did not understand a great deal. It was just that he had more to understand.

As he left, prepared to walk to the right past the window of naked chickens, the little man gave him an envelope made of rice paper, probably from Shantung.

· 4 ·

What was in it for him?

He sat on a newspaper, the Sunday *Mail*, at the beach just east of Adelaide. The prepositions were defining his life now. Why was he in South Australia?

His fingers acted nearly independently in the tan sand, picking little clam shells out of their rest, picking up the long screw shells with no corresponding name in his memory. He was not idle, or he did not feel comfortable enough to sense himself as idle, but he was sitting on the beach. His fingers could have been diddling for gold nuggets. The beach was called Henley. It went left and right, probably north and south, for miles. He would have to turn over a lot of sand to find any gold, perhaps a coin lost by an English sailor in 1792, perhaps a clue.

He felt somewhat clever for a second, but not very clever then. He was understanding more, but there was all the time more to understand, February at Henley Beach.

To his left a young woman with a very dark naked back because it was nearly the end of summer was enwrapped with a sullen youth, probably a smash shop worker. It was Sunday.

How long was he supposed to sit here, the jetty to his right? If he gave up he had no reason not to go back across the dateline, into yesterday.

There were many people with dogs on the beach, though there were not many people on the beach. But they were all kinds of dogs.

Then there she was, the woman with the black and white Newfoundland. Best in the show. He was sort of determined to ask for an explanation. If this one were killed on the premises, how could he go on?

She did not even approach him. But the dog came over, black and white on the tan, folded paper in his mouth. It was truly silly. The dog dropped the paper in the sand, nodded its head, and leapt into a turn. The woman was running in the sea breeze. It was cool enough to make one wear a shirt.

He picked up the paper and unfolded it. A brochure for the Festival of Perth.

· 5 ·

Details, yes, particulars, indeed.

The blue bruise on the neck of the woman in the casket, of course, just visible despite silk around her neck. Each detail complete for the moment one regards it, another peanut in the can of Nobbys salted mixed nuts. Yes. But details are only something, and one can notice them all the time one is awake.

Is there an earthquake here in Perth right now? Not enough details are known. What kind of meat was that on the tray during the TAA flight?

The more certain details are, the less likely they are to be the greatest matters. It would take all the details on every continent and then some, he thought, as he took a sip of Swan Lager, to add up to complete understanding.

The greatest matters lie beyond death, beyond the stars, in the aorta of time. A corpse is a detail. A second of starlight, even from the mid-Pacific sky full of stars, is a detail. No matter how many details he might acquire, he would never arrive at truth here on the Indian Ocean.

No matter. He would settle for a little more knowledge. Let understanding come when it choose.

He had a copy of the program for the Festival of Perth. What was he to attend to find another detail or two? Igor Oistrakh and Leonid Block were going to play a lot of Paganini, including more than one Caprice. Was that a clue from Russia or simply an enticing title? *Koyaanisqatsi* was playing, but everything in that could be misconstrued as a message. The Nylons would be there. He had seen them in Toronto the night after his dinner at the Thai restaurant on Bloor Street West.

He would go to hear the Nylons.

Probably it didnt matter where he went. They would find him.

But no, they probably wanted him to look for a pattern of details in the words.

He would probably one day understand some small matters.

All this prattle about understanding.

Call it intelligence. All the knowledge he could pick up would not add up to intelligence. All the learning he managed to do would not amount to understanding. Acquaintance with a great number of details might keep him alive, but it wouldnt guarantee that he would know why.

Walking out into the sultry night air after the Nylons concert, he told himself for the fiftieth time, look right when you step into the street, the drivers dont know you're a North American. The long terrifying Pacific 747 trip had receded into a second of regard. He was on solid ground, not an earthquake since the night before.

He did not step into the street, St. George's Terrace. He would hang around for a minute or two, like a U.S. sailor off detail. Maybe they meant *after* the Nylons.

They?

Standing around, his leathern bag over his shoulder, was no great fun, sweat pouring down his side, bumping over his ribcage. There were blisters on his feet in the loafers.

While he stood there a woman at the Western Australia Institute of Technology phoned his hotel room. The light on his telephone was a yellowish orange.

He saw a sailor walking unsteadily along the sidewalk on the odd-number side of the street. The sailor was not wearing a uniform, but he was wearing navy shoes and a navy haircut.

Two years ago he had read an article on Perth in the *National Geographic*. In the article it was said that the sailors of the U.S. Navy had voted Perth their favourite shore liberty in the world.

Navy shoes and navy haircut. That was an observation. It

became knowledge, or nearly so. It did not advance him a step toward understanding. Still he followed the sailor, what direction he did not know.

· 7 ·

The sailor had had nothing to do with it, or so it seemed, or he had had nothing to do with it directly. He maintained that he was John Quadra from California. Maybe.

Saying goodbye in the morning, he had given over a schedule of events for the literary segment of the Festival, a few days of lectures and readings at the new State Library, a list of artistic disquisitions.

It made sense for an American sailor to divest himself of a program of writers' talks, but it seemed odd that he would possess such a thing in the first place.

At nine in the morning it was already over thirty degrees and the previous night's *Daily News* promised forty for this afternoon. The salon at the library was air conditioned. He decided to give it a try. The gift had been a printed message, after all. But this was all senseless; how could a woman on a street corner in North America signify anything congruent with a passing mariner in Western Australia? Paper is passed between hands every micro-second anywhere in the logos.

Talk talk talk, wave of applause. He had heard many men and women discourse into a microphone or a darkness, and he had never heard one convinced or even aware of the knowledge that wisdom is not the sum of learning.

A middle-aged man in a teenager's poetry suit was offering platitudes in rime between pell-mell bursts of patter in a nearly indecipherable antipodean version of British bluster. The audience cracked into appreciation each time a jest was half-swallowed or a quatrain resolved in a whimsical rebel

14

aphorism. No wisdom here, but the air conditioning was working and the seats were new and a little comfortable.

Knowledge crept along for a few hours, and then it was time for lunch.

· 8 ·

Lunch was a dismal sandwich of some unrecognizable flesh and white bread, and what they called here 'brewed coffee,' no beer in the cafeteria at the library.

Chewing on his sandwich, idly scanning the room for the naked skin so prevalent in Perth, he eventually departed into his own mind. He remembered nothing said by the man poet or the woman novelist. He retreated into his own mind. He moved around in it, searching for something stable. He saw a piece of Hong Kong silk around a blue neck, but that was only memory, too recent to be memory, perhaps, a glimpse of a future memory.

He looked assiduously around in his mind, among the memories, as his teeth ground an unknown animal. Maybe a marsupial. He searched what some people called himself.

We are trained to consider our own skin, all surface, hair, nails, warts, as something exterior to ourselves.

He looked with persistence around the corners and niches in his mind. Really, when you considered carefully, you might easily be persuaded that this extreme westward trip was hallucinatory. If it is not indeed a dream, the cause of it might be interior. Was the woman in Seattle really the woman in Toronto? Did he have any business looking at that dead flesh in Sydney? In the newspaper it was reported that the temperature was thirty degrees cooler than the air across a continent in Perth. Very unusual, the persistence of the old century, they said to him.

15

Was it really dead flesh? Was it reasonable, if the brain had been dead for a short time, to say that the flesh was dead?

Had he spent all that money travelling here after a puzzle that could have been solved inside his own cranial globe? Was he sitting fecklessly in this new internationally-styled library building, waiting for a clue that he could have invented in his apartment at forty-nine degrees north?

A tea cup rattled. A chair scraped a table. The English short story writer was even now being introduced in the auditorium.

· 9 ·

The English short story writer had come as far as he had, though from the other direction, but had presumably come on a mission clearly sane.

If, that is, writing down stories can be considered rational, if flying around the world to a big slab of brown land in the southern ocean to read to a hundred people what one has written may be considered temperate behaviour.

If the local can be found regularly over the blue globe, it is the general condition of the local that any person living there will seek rest in his mind.

It would seem almost to be natural, the natural condition of people before their short story is told. If a person could look around clearly in his own head, he should see sanity, he should encounter order. He might be home in the rainforest, sweeping snow off his front steps.

He thought it was time to go home.

The English short story writer was reading a story out loud. She said she had seen the young man in the Thai restaurant in Rome.

16

When she had finished reading, she began talking with a cluster of chittering West Australian women. When she was finished doing that, she went out into the bright humid air through which one could see white concrete, and got into a taxi that had been standing in the street beside a heap of shaped paving bricks. He got into the taxi with her.

He didnt know why. He didnt know his own mind.

· 10 ·

But it seemed as if she did.

He found out that she was not as young as she had looked on the podium. Her hair was shot with grey, and her small breasts hung against her. But she was welcoming and her body was cool along its limbs in the hot night of the Indian Ocean. She was just a year younger than he was, but she was older, she was English, her voice was quiet while they made love in the room overlooking the swimming pool, but her body was noisy, and the logos, it was noisy. She was English grammar gone native, and he was not a writer, but for a while he was a verb and she was his subject.

If the travelling here, west as he would ever go, was crazy, this moment was pure sanity, his flesh refusing to soften in her, their perspiration making them as slick outside as inside. And he knew that sanity was the dream of the logos, he knew the temperance after their ride beneath the southern constellations was the demand a holy order would make.

They did not even shower. They rang room service for swim suits, the young woman at the door declared the raiment to be 'swimmers,' and they went down to the pool and jumped in, splash, two predicates under water where lights looked at them as if they were fish.

When they reached one another they looked into each other's eyes for truth, and then they spoke it. What they said

17

was not knowledge, it was wisdom in the cool air beneath the warm air.

They clung together in the water, but they did not become water themselves. They knew a great many particulars of each other, separate as they were. They gave heed.

· 11 ·

Keep your eyes open, keep your ears open, get ready to learn something at any moment, even if it will not lead to wisdom.

Till you get to wisdom, maybe, keep your mouth shut. He had said a lot of unmemorable things to her after the pool, and now there were considerable stretches of time about which he could not remember anything. But she was the English short story writer, giving heed while he gave what was left of his head. There were brains in his head, still, and words in her heart, and some day she might write them for him, or for someone.

She was sanity, all right. He said let me follow you around the world, and she replied get home. She made love with him again, on the spongy Australian grass, but then she repeated: get home.

He was not home, not yet. He was trying to recover from long plane flights and from her, in a Holiday Inn among a tangle of U.S. freeway overpasses, between an airport and a house-spattered tropic hill, where the Babylonians had whored away paradise.

Now he appreciated Murray Bail's lantern-jawed Aussies, who deserved a better reputation. They may wear khaki shorts over hairy legs, and swill tinned beer in jeeps, but their cities look more like ordered coastlines than this Budweiser Honolulu. Two hours ago he had ducked in for a piss in a rotting bar that smelled like putrified fish and met the oncoming darkness with a scurry of cockroaches.

18

Who would have thought?

In the restaurant at the Holiday Inn it was no holiday. For the tenth day in a row he ordered the wrong thing, and then he watched the sergeant. He could hear only the crying and banging children behind him, but he had a clear line of sight on the sergeant.

The sergeant sat down after he did, and left before he did. He wore one of those U.S. military uniforms that look like a video game. His face he placed a few inches over his fruit cocktail, and the latter was gone. Soup gone. He wrapped his fist around a verticle fork stuck into a steak and with a knife he cut it, then switched hands and jammed it in. He wore stylish glasses but his short straw hair stuck up here and there. He had a big Coca Cola with his steak. He ate five buttered rolls. He ate everything and didnt leave a tip. He was gone.

· 12 ·

Sitting in the cafeteria at LAX, looking out a window at painted steel tails moving past, hearing cross-currents of Spanish, Chinese, American and Muzak, he reflected on what he had seen in the past two weeks, lots of writing, white beaches, little globules of water on a naked shoulder.

He had heard lots, too, but most of that he could not remember, and what he could remember he could not depend on. He read about weddings in the Los Angeles *Times.* He kept nudging his shoulder bag with his ankle. He was back across the Pacific Ocean all right at least.

Even what she had said just after his best moment and just before hers. It was a short story in a British accent, or so it seemed, and fiction is not as dependable as something you can see. So he thought.

Well, he knew a little Spanish, and in a lull of the Chinese he heard a little Spanish say 'matado al sitio.'

But when he turned to look, he did not see a little Mexican, male or female. Maybe there was one there, but he didnt see one. He saw the usual sixty-year-old American with his pot belly and golf hat and fifty-eight-year-old wife with marcelled hair and cardigan sweater. They were discussing golf in Tucson, in American.

He didnt want to, but he could easily believe his eyes.

Still, he would watch for a little Mexican or a little Guatemalan getting onto Western Airlines Flight 465 bound for Vancouver.

· 13 ·

On the plane he was all hunger and no appetite.

He could not put the meat they plunked before him into his mouth. He felt as if all the meals he had eaten in Boeing 727s were just generic food, different coloured things he had picked out of their cute containers and shoved into the largest hole in the front of his head. There his eating was as bad as his handwriting had become. The longer he lived this way the further he descended the social order, the more he flew away from the earth the further back he retreated through the pathway of human civilization.

He read *Time* magazine instead of a novel. The man across from him was wearing a corduroy suit and was almost finished Sisson's translation of Lucretius. He would know literate man's ordering of mute nature. Probably a novice flyer.

He sat in yesterday's underwear and socks. He stuck Life-Savers into his mouth and concealed scraps of the wrapping paper around the seats.

20

He closed his eyes and let his head loll in full view of a hundred and fifty people. He farted in the cover of the engine roar and the jet of overhead air. He took his shoes off and wiggled his toes through the holes in his fetid socks. He was going home.

He sprawled in *techne*'s floral-printed chair and allowed himself to become a barbarian.

Over the past two weeks he had felt as if there were a sequence of messages and gestures directed intentionally toward him, a woman in a Thai restaurant, words over a shop window in a city he would be unlikely ever to walk through.

Now surrounded by strangers in an aluminum tube high in the air, he would not see or hear a most obvious sign. Not even illuminated words about a seat belt buckle. His eyes and ears were useless now, and knowledge dropped away behind the wobbling craft.

· 14 ·

All the time he was home he talked and acted as if he were asleep.

The ancients and the more recent ancients were never fortunate enough to see their great cities from the sky. London, say, flat London. A spry eighteenth-century boy might stand straight up on the roof of St. Paul's and see the streets stretch away, but he could not cruise over the whole city and see its famous marks displayed as a plan all at once.

But they never experienced jet lag, either. They might be vomitous every day of the long passage across the Atlantic, but they never crossed two oceans in less than a week. They never crossed one ocean on a whim.

At home in Vancouver he looked at the Patti Page record that had warped in his suitcase, and then when he tried to find a friend's number in the phone book, say his friend was named Bill Horseman, he found himself looking under P. It was the wrong page. He was acting as if he were asleep.

In the bathroom he drank half a glass of water and poured the other half out on the sinkboard, where it found its way to the edge. He might have been asleep.

Acting as if one is asleep and talking like a sleeping person can make one sound as if one were completely without learning, a barbarian. It can make you seem vulnerable, or it can make you vulnerable.

But in the few days he was there he managed to sell some things for quite a lot of money, and buy other things at a rather good price. He could do that in his sleep.

But now, or rather then, sitting sleepily in Dora's Café, where he got a bargain, he realized that the English short story writer had not suggested that he get home. She had said go to Rome. He replayed her inflected voice in his barely waking ear. Yes, she had said 'Geh t'Rome.'

Waiting in the lounge at Heathrow, while doing as he was bid, he had seen her picture on the back of a book in someone's hands. An Italian was sitting in such a way as not to ruin the crease in his slacks in the smoking section, ostentatiously reading this book.

In the photograph one could not see the grey hairs. He was in love with an English woman but her photograph was just a picture. In love. Oh no. Oh probably yes.

· 15 ·

In the lounge at Heathrow he put down the copy of *The Times* he had found, and looked at the human beings coming through the gates.

What a lot of human beings there were. He was sleepy after seeing three oceans in six days, but he was awake, looking at all the human beings who had come here to London on airplanes.

As they walked by, carrying as many pieces of hand-luggage as they could, he watched them and made guesses as to their homes. He thought he saw lots of Germans, and in fact he did. He heard them speaking their fascinating language, a little more gentle than it had been in all the movies of his youth.

He thought about how he liked the language he used with himself, but how he would be embarrassed by it if other human beings could hear it, or read it. That would be the worst, if they could read it. Well, they would never read it.

Germans, Japanese, Italians. All the movies of his youth. As long as he could stay awake, smoking an American cigarette, sitting on this black woven fabric, he would share a world with them. They were inside a kind of soundproof glass.

An Australian was waiting for the same plane he would be taking to Rome. He thought at first that this human being with the bushman hat, blue jeans, outback boots, and red and white scarf with the word 'ROO' all over it, was a man about forty-five years of age. Then he thought he saw mounds in the sweater and thought it might be an Australian woman. He remembered that he used to think that Australian women looked like men in women's clothes. That was before he had been in Perth. This one had medium long hair and a deep voice when she spoke to the Englishman in the Italian sweater. But she was wearing men's clothes. And she had words on her.

Arabs, Africans, Americans with Irish tweed hats. As long as he could stay awake he would share the world with all of them, knowledge showing in their purposeful walking, even in the bickering tired families.

23

On the Super 737 over the rain storm on top of the Alps he fell asleep and missed his meal. His mind was gone.

After he was finally able to show the cab driver how to get to Viale Gorizia and the Hotel Fenix, he stayed awake long enough to set his portable radio to Roman music. Then he dropped the back of his head onto the white linen and cascaded into sleep again. He went for hours and hours into a private world. No one else was there. He dreamed of the corpse in Sydney, but she too was in a world of her own.

· 16 ·

Now he would see whether the written messages would continue to find him, and if they did, whether they would be written in English or Italian, or Latin, or something previous to that.

His eyes were closed more than usual, and behind them rolled the waters of three oceans. Having been in seventeen time zones in a week, he knew he had to pick up seventeen extra hours of sleep. So he turned out the bedlight at the Fenix at eleven, and woke to Roman music at eight. While he slept he saw dreams. An English woman lay her body on him and took his breath away. He woke up to breathe.

While awake he saw death. Not death in a Sydney casket but a dying world. The bare trees of the Via Nomentana led him where the No. 16 autobus wanted to go. On the first day it took him to the little station, where he got off, an American magazine full of English words rolled in his hand, and walked between large coloured Italian words until he stopped and turned and found himself in front of the famous number 26, high on a wall.

He ducked inside the door, a contradictory figure, climbed the steps, rang the bell, was admitted, found himself surrounded by books full of words, went to the last little room in the corner, here in the Northern Hemisphere. There was no bed because after the poet had died his landlady had had to burn it. But one could still look at the ceiling the poet looked at with his last eyes. There was no reason to look at it twice. It was blue and the designs were white or gold. Who remembers after death?

After death the second day he went by grimy subway, past hidden artifacts, to the Colosseum and the scattered remnants of the Forum. Messages left by the energetic but dead.

He looked into the eyes of the wandering strangers, even some of the Japanese. No communications. Some screaming American children ran toward him on the staircase. He told them in English to shut up.

In the Canadian magazine he carried this day he read about a youth who bequeathed death to his family. The youth said that he got messages from everywhere.

– I got this message that I had to kill my family.

He was diagnosed. They gave him drugs to make him dream.

· 17 ·

Sometimes the ears are more reliable witnesses than are the eyes.

Finally that night, after thinking about it for two days, he dropped his glasses onto the marble floor and broke them. In the morning he took his glasses to the eyeglasses store, and when he came back to the hotel that afternoon he found that they had moved him to a new room with a textured rug on the floor. His life had always been filled with if only. If only he had chosen Vietnamese food that night instead of Thai food.

25

Now with his other glasses on he felt giddy, the lenses were not quite right, he took them off to write a letter to the English short story writer. He wanted to tell her that he had looked for her in the presence of death this morning, down where the light bulbs were faint in the catacombs leading to Ste. Agnes. It was always eve down there. He had looked for her and he had looked for an interesting name in the Protestant graveyard just outside the crumbled gates of the city. He knew that it was not likely that she would be back in England, but he supposed that the letter he was writing while standing in the Ostiense post office might never get there anyway.

With his glasses off he saw the first sign of spring, a pink or purple glow outside where the rain was ceasing. He put on his unsatisfactory old glasses and looked at the Japanese plum trees ragged in bloom. All along Nomentana Street the tall trees were still bare, and he had misplaced all thought of spring. Now here it was, come out of hiding. He saw four teenaged human beings leaping up to break loose a twig of pink or purple blossoms each. He was a little annoyed.

But then as he walked the streets and then as he rode the subway back to the terminal, he saw twigs of green-yellow blossoms in people's hands, not just young women, but short old men as well. It was March 8, International Women's Day. A day for nature to become, if one could only see, if one had eyes to witness.

He did not know where in the world she was, but the earth was there between their feet.

· 18 ·

Well yes, the Eternal City, but what is an eternal city in a world that changes minute by minute, that dies before our eyes and is gone forever, but is there anything forever, even gone?

Eternal verities, if there ever were such things, are going to be hard to find on a ground that is being pulled out from under you, he thought, walking out of la Chiesa di Saint Peter in Chains and looking out over the little square on top of a hill. He had been looking at Michelangelo's Moses, so solid, heavy, seated with such immovability, such huge feet. Michelangelo liked huge hands and huge feet and bulging veins. Such solidity. On its way out.

So what a world to be looking for a message in. It would have to be a passing word, from the dead to the dying. But if you are in the middle of the wind, the wind is standing still, no? If you are short-sighted because your glasses were not yet repaired.

Had he been thinking of the truth back there in Australia? Is a message of necessity the truth? For a madman, killer or not, it is. Are we talking about a message of necessity or the necessity of truth? Did we come to Rome to talk like this?

He saw a German-looking woman in a camel-hair cape looking at him more than is usual among passing travellers. If she had some spoken or printed words for him, she would have to approach. He was not going to approach. He had been given sanity by the fiction smithy in Perth, and he was not about to test it here. He had not even looked for words in the configuration of Peter's chains lit behind glass under the altar of the church, that focal point. If ever a message – let the Italian Catholics read that.

He was not in Rome to look for a miracle or an oracle, but he was lonely for intentional strangers. He gave a cigarette to anyone who asked for one in the street.

The oracle at the altar does not tell you anything in any way different from nature or the succession of street signs. He does not explain anything and he does not obscure anything. He simply offers a symbol. A cat on a grave, a ring

around a cloud. A score on page three of *Il Corriere dello Sport:*
Juventus 3, Sparta Prago 0.

The German-looking woman was walking toward the
very old stairway down to the street. Well, he was going that
way.

· 19 ·

– Ah, she said, in accented English, that was heaven. This
is heaven.

– What, he said.

– Heaven, she repeated. To be in Rome, and to be in bed
with sore feet and a body covered with sweat. Is it all right to
say this, sweat?

– All right, he said.

– And you too, she said. I dont know which is your sweat
and which is my.

– Mine, he said.

– Mine, you are mine. This day, in any case. You are my
angel in this heaven Rome, and if you believe it, Annalise is
yours.

– A na lease?

– Anna Lise.

– No, he said. I mean about heaven. We are creatures with
fallen souls, with earthly desires.

Later she held what appeared to be his salsiccia in her cool
hand and it began to recover.

– I do not displeasure you with my earthy desire, she
whispered in his ear. Then she finished her declarative sentence with the point of her tongue.

– Heaven cannot be what we desire, he said. It is not logical. Our human desires and even our human imaginations
are incapable of knowing even a little of what heaven is.

Therefore heaven must be what we do not want. We will not be able to understand it when we see it.

–Logic in bed, she said. Are you sure you are not a German?

–I am only a fallen creature of the world, looking for truth, he said.

– Look at this, she said. This is truth.

–No, that is nice, but it is not truth. Truth is more difficult to find, and it comes so quickly one does not understand it.

– Are you saying that Annalise was too easy to attain?
She let go.

–No, I loved attaining you, he said. I would like to attain you again. It is just that I was hoping, silly, I know, I was just hoping that you might have a message for me.

She let her crinkled blonde hair fall over her face, and slid down his body.

–Here is a message for you, she said, and she continued to utter sounds in her throat, but they were indecipherable.

2 · Stay Going

In the morning at the hotel's little bar he always had what everyone else was having, a plain brioche and a coffee.

He always asked for caffe latte in the morning and capuccino at night; it had been his habit for years. But you could always drink it so fast, usually standing up. After less than a week he found himself longing for the kind of sit-down coffee he got at home. He found an image curling in his mind's eye. He was letting a little cream spill into the middle of a wide cup of black coffee, and before it turned the coffee brown, it began to spin, cream colour spinning heavy in the coffee.

The immense earth was between his feet and the floor he had stood on two weeks ago in Honolulu. Yet in half a day he would be under that sky over the Pacific, the surface of the earth spinning a thousand miles an hour.

The electrons inside the cream inside his mind's eye were spinning faster. Out there a galaxy was spinning so that it trailed a swath of stars like a lawn sprinkler trailing beads of water that spin themselves to the green grass.

Everything spins.

The total amount of spin in the spinning universe remains the same. The only thing that does.

The strolling Italian pedestrians, eyes always turned another direction, spin off one another as they go, somewhere down Via Nazionale.

Each time he was nudged on one side he would go with the consequent turn, and there it would be, another possible street.

He spun off Annalise, he thought, into the arms of Annalise, who had herself been turned.

Aye, and she will turn again. The eternal citizen, spinning like knowledge, and he knew he was foolish to think that no one else knew about this. Knew more than he did. Someone must, if only because he knew so little more than he had known in the Thai restaurant.

But he knew Annalise, knew her and knew her. It was as if he had always known her. On the table beside his bed was a square piece of paper. In print it said Keats-Shelley Memorial, Piazza di Spagna, 26, Roma, Admission L.2000, No. 14814. In ink it had the 2000 corrected to 2500, and in the leftover white space, it said Altensteinstrasse.

The writer was, again, departed.

· 21 ·

He descended along the old stone street, his head spinning, down the Spanish steps, his feet hitting like spondees, down the Via Condotti, around the jog, down the Via Tomacelli, to the Lungotevere.

He had been here a week but never before seen the river. Caesar had never seen it either. If he was going to jump in from the Ponte Cavour he had better do it right now, he thought.

Too late. The river was gone, another river never seen by Caesar was there, but he no longer was, but now he was a changed man.

He would give up looking for messages. He had no idea where Altensteinstrasse might be. He would simply become what he secretly was, a tourist, not a traveller. He would buy a new map. It would show where the rivers and the streets used to go.

He looked across the bridge toward the dome in the haze. He thought the haze was an expression of his earthly desires. He wished he could start over and wholly see.

· 22 ·

While packing his bags quickly for the flight to Europe he had been thinking of space.

Should I take an umbrella, should I take a sweater. No, it is really spring, isnt it, and I am going to Sunny Italy. Isnt it?

In Rome it was raining, and when the clouds wandered away it became cold, and in his hotel room it was cold in the late afternoon. He remembered his hotel room in Perth, in which the air conditioning did not really work. Now he wished he had an umbrella and a sweater. Even when he was not really wet any more he felt wet because inside the black leather jacket he was cold. What about spring, yes what about his Roman spring, mister?

But fall will come to Perth, eventually, and spring will come to Rome. Cool streets will become warm. The sun will glow off almost gold stones as in the magazines. Wet side-walks will lose their puddles and become dusty. The world's world will spin, and so will she, and so will his blood, it will spin about his body and limbs.

His body ached a little, not now his traveller's feet and back, but the parts awakened by Annalise, the long German who wrote her story on his body before she spun out of his life.

Her perspiration had eventually dried from his body and

33

hers, their temperatures had cooled, and now they were probably a country or two apart. A good thing.

Naturally when he woke to find her gone he checked all his money and things. If anything, he had more now than ever. But probably he had the same.

He had not jumped into any of the rivers that passed. In the guide book written by an American Jew it said that the Tiber was a continuous present given to agriculturist and traveller alike. A smart lady, an altenstein from the new world.

He was hungry. He would, because he could find no Thai restaurant, go out in the rain in search of a place prepared to present some *carne calda*.

· 23 ·

The following morning he gave up and purchased an umbrella for 11,000 lire at the train station.

Now he would be prepared for the changes in the weather. Unsettled, they called this sort of thing back home. It was begining to look as if it would be like this for a while. He was more or less resigned to the fact that the only thing he could depend on was change.

–It is not usually like this at this time of the year, said the man behind the desk in the lobby.

–I have learned to expect that wherever I go in the world, he replied. He was leaving for downtown.

Still, he decided to go to the Vatican, rain or no rain. If there was one island of stability in the volatile world, it was the Pontificate. No one could abridge that. But one could say just the opposite. His dull measured life of days would be arrested and a thrill enter his memory on his first visit to the basilica of Saint Peter. You cant win.

Win? You cant say anything that will remain what you said. If only he were an English short story writer, he would find a way to make that interesting. He would begin with observations in the Metro car on the way to Ottaviano station. The short woman who was holding onto the same stanchion he was gripping. She had wide crude features but she did not have the rest of the characteristics he had learned to associate with such a face in the past week. She was wearing her coarse black hair tied in a tail that decreased in thickness as the knots descended her back. She had a smart pea-jacket, and a bag over one shoulder, unlike most of the Roman women, who wore theirs across the body to discourage purse-snatchers. She was wearing olive leather slacks and new narrow loafers. She was holding her hand low on the stanchion. He was developing a little tumescence. When the train stopped gently for the Lepanto station, he let his body give with the brakes, and his little hardness tapped against her plump knuckles. Faces in the crowd. She stepped away a little when some people got off, holding the stanchion a little higher, her arm outstretched. Was she removing herself or making herself more visible? An apparition.

There's a message for *you*, he thought. You can begin to wonder whether it came on purpose.

In an alcove at the basilica he read the names of the popes from Peter to John Paul, carved into a giant slab. Each had touched the former and the follower. There was continuity. There was a message passed on.

· 24 ·

Perhaps that first woman in the Thai restaurant was Italian.

Perhaps he should look for a Thai woman in an Italian restaurant. But no, here they were all Italian restaurants, and there they are not all Thai restaurants. In fact they are hardly ever Thai restaurants. Maybe he should look for a Thai woman in a Canadian restaurant in Rome. On the other hand, on the knuckles of that hand, in any case, there were lots of Oriental women around town, and not just the young Japanese tourists. He kept his eye on them, especially as he was entering and exiting restaurants, and especially he had kept his eye on this one, because she had a Fiat. But why all these women? There was a sailor man of the Indian Ocean, yes, but why all these women, including the dead one or the dead ones. Yes, but they started it, or that first one did.

It turned out that she had a small flat over a shop on the end of the Villa Pescheria in Viterbo. How nice. There was melted snow on the Medieval streets in Viterbo, and on her patio above the shop, but how nice. What an amazing place to be, he thought, looking at her short brown leg thrown over a jumble of white sheets that had been crisp at first.

Viterbo was inside a high wall. The narrow twisty streets were steep on the hillside. Each piece had been added to earlier pieces, and then eight hundred years later along came the Fiat. Under all of it spread the galleries opened in the earth by the Etruscans. This was not getting him anywhere. She did not speak English and he did not speak Italian or Thai.

They, like Viterbo, were developments in the accidental accumulations of history. History was a child making castles on the beach or against a mountainside. All the inventions and power of the human race were the moment-by-moment whims of that kid in the sand.

He looked out the window at the steep back of an abandoned church with no roof. He could buy it if he wanted to. Some hand had neglected it, or some war had removed it, it made no difference now.

He wanted to say all this to Signorina Lotus Blossom, but

36

she woke and said things to him in another language that he was learning quickly. Like a child among foreigners.

All right, he said, joining with feigned enthusiasm in the conversation, among the wet petals. But I am tired of all this, all these women. He hoped she would not drive him back to Rome, eighty-five kilometers away. He would be satisfied with the train station, the bus station.

· 25 ·

The old joke held that among the world's shortest books is a very thin volume called *Italian War Heroes*.

But the Italians desire heroes, yes they do. They sometimes make do with Hadrian, sometimes with Paulo Rossi. No soldiers strike as heroic poses as the muscular Italian fusilier taking a forward-leaning stride, rifle in one hand, bugle in the other. This is a huge piece of dark metal from World War I, of course. It is not easy to find curios of Mussolini's soldier. He has disappeared from history.

Cavour and Garibaldi are around, though. History has decided to make them sand castles with no waves in sight.

The Italians have not been at war for forty years, he thought, riding silently in the right front seat of the little faded red Fiat. But without war there would be no Italy. Does that mean it is already disappearing before our eyes?

Ruby Foo looked at him and smiled with her lips closed. She took his silence for sadness that their campaign was over.

Without an adversary you cannot be strong, cannot finally be at all. War built the Forum and the Great Wall of China. No one can find a monument in Iceland. War discloses personal fate.

Ruby reached over with her right hand and stroked him where he was sore, driving with her eyes on the road and her mouth, as it always was except when she was smiling, open.

37

He could not remember his life before a month and a half ago. The woman in the Toronto restaurant – had she been a little Asiatic, a little Italian, southern, perhaps, a dark German? Were they all counters in a game of chance? Surely not, surely there was some person or some organization of people interested in him.

Were they using him or were they employing him? Was there some struggle in whose course he was essential? Why did they seek him out? What was there in his life before a month and a half ago that made him interesting to them?

War is the son of the kid on the beach and the father of our father. His father had walked well in front of the American soldiers up the Italian boot forty years ago. Had he been in Viterbo?

Suzy Wong had found his hotel before he had recognized the neighbourhood. She smiled with her lips closed and patted his ass as he peeled the little Fiat off himself. He patted his jacket to reassure himself that he was still carrying his wallet.

· 26 ·

He could not find a Thai restaurant in Rome.

But after Sunday noon mass at Santa Maria Maggiore, he went down a steep side street and found a Sezchuan restaurant. There was not enough pique in the piccante, but it was nice to be using chopsticks again rather than twirling a fork.

Shortly after he sat down, two people sat at his table, because the little place was filling up with Catholics. Beside him sat a man and across from him a slim nun in a well-cut dark grey habit and sharp eyeglasses. She was thin and beautiful and wealthy-looking, with perfect white teeth and a darting pink tongue. It was startling because she was a nun, and these people were from the Indian part of Asia some-where. Goa?

In the hubbub of the small restaurant he tried to hear their language. Most of the time he could not hear it. Portuguese? But when they ordered their food she spoke what sounded like perfect Italian, with that high pitch you hear from Indian women. The man's lower voice danced around in that fashion that humourists love in Indian-inflected English.

God, he would love to be able to hear her, whether there were a message here or not, but the babble of languages bounced off every surface in the little place – Italian, English, Chinese, Japanese, probably Latin. No Spanish to say matado in sitio, though he had seen two separate young women in the church, carrying Spanish-language guide books.

But it was this beautiful Brahmin bride of Christ who fascinated him. She wore a gold watch and a gold ring, and her fine features were perfect.

She was, whatever she was, something he had never imagined, and he imagined whoever was imagining him finding the closest thing he could to a Thai restaurant and putting him there just for such a discovery.

Whatever she was, she was a beautiful and confident arti-fact of the world, fallen though it be. Indian, Christian, Roman, she was the product of strife in some part of the world east. An artifact, yes, but fashioned out of war in an eastern part of the world, war that has always been the natural condition of human life.

If there is justice it is created by war. If there is beauty it has been put at our table by war.

He wanted to talk to her, but she was a nun, and he didnt have the language, probably, and there was the man in the bomber jacket beside him.

In the morning, three days short of the spring equinox, there was an enormous snowfall.

Big fluffy snowflakes turned the cypress trees outside his balcony window white. The snow was so thick that the clogged traffic along the Via Nomentana retreated from continual horn-blowing to intermittent horn-blowing.

He stood naked at his window and looked at the amazing spring snow. A couple weeks ago in Perth they had told him the record heat wave was of course highly unusual. Now he lifted his gaze to the left and saw that the entire continent of Europe was being covered with snow. Snow is supposed to be peaceful. Or Lieutenant Henry said that in the Italian mountains war could not proceed in the snow.

But this snow was foreboding, a little frightening. It was spring, after all, and this Rome. He thought about the fashionable phrase, 'nuclear winter.' A girl telling her parent, yes, she did remember summer, it happened when she was a little child learning to walk, no it must have been later, there was earth, wasnt there.

As the snow fell resolutely, he imagined being inside the luxurious church he had visited yesterday – Santa Maria Maggiore.

In the night of August 5th, 352 A.D., the Virgin appeared in a dream to the patrician John and to Pope Liberius, commanding them to build a church on the spot where on the following day snow would fall. The miracle took place and the basilica was erected.

August 6th. That would be Hiroshima's day. Fire and Ice.

Snow is not the only thing to fall from the sky. Fire falls too, must fall if ice will fall. But fire wants to rise, it will rise again. Or all things will come to an end, down to nothing, the last smoke spinning into the space where there was still air.

Trying to get a handle on the Mediterranean, he had started with Homer. Homer knew about strife, but in the *Iliad*, xviii. 107, he had forgotten the way of the sea, and uttered the wish that gods and lesser beings might forget war. It was still a popular sentiment today, uttered from human minds that owed their existence to strife. Dante and his church knew better.

Yes, so he would go out and make footprints in the snow, and let them follow him, whoever they were.

3 · Going with Nature

While drinking his customary caffe latte and eating his plain cornetto in the hotel bar the next morning, he heard a man's voice offer a sepulchral 'buon giorno.'

He was an Italian who looked like a German, with his light brown hair and tweed outdoors cap. This contradictory individual took a cigarette out of a pack on which in strictly erect letters was printed the brand name, STOP. As he snapped his ebon lighter, one's eyes fixed upon the sudden flame, and one felt as if the fire were everything in the world, or at least the focus of the spinning logos. The universe all flocks to a fiery roost.

St. Peter's ashes in the Vatican. The ashes of Mark the Evangelist in S.M. Maggiore. Nero's blackened city under the pavement. The Canadian soldiers sacrificed to the German flames by General Mark Clark before he marched his clean Americans into the motion picture liberation of Rome. Etna and Vesuvius spouting fiery earth to feed the olive orchards of the future. The fiery sun was out this morning, melting the last of the snow in the Forum. A fair exchange.

He took the number 36 bus as he did every day, down to the station, thence to descend past ashes to the Metro and into the ancient region or the shopping piazzi.

The traveller thinks all day of the money in his pocket. He is always looking for a fair exchange he can understand. If he does not convert thousands into dollars the money will burn a hole in his pocket.

Everything becomes fire. Everything becomes lire. A fair exchange admits no liar.

While crossing the Piazza di Spagna he saw a slim Japanese girl in red shining boots. She was just doing her last calculations on a little black hand calculator as she walked where the Fiats could not go, over the cobbles. She snapped the little thing closed and put it in her purse. She did not smile or frown. She must have got a fair exchange.

He followed her into a snack bar with shiny tubes running horizontal and vertical. As she ordered a Coca Cola he ordered a beer. He noticed that beer cans in Australia and Italy both proclaimed sponsorship of their 1987 America's Cup boats. An expensive business. The winners of a boat race on the Thames are tradition-bound to burn their craft to the water line.

He lit a cigarette. The Japanese girl was staring, in the mirror wall, into the flame.

· 29 ·

She was different far from any other person, any other woman.

But the fire in her loins was the fire that tore the earth from the sun.

No man had a hand in the creation. No god could have stood up to the flame.

—If you cant stand the heat, he said when she came for him a third time, stay out of the kitchen.

She giggled and then so did her entire body.

—Kitchen, she said then. And laughed. This is not your kitchen, Yankee.

I'm not a Yankee, he was going to say, but it was too late for speech.

They kindled again and subsided again, just like the universe.

– In the great project of gathering intelligence, he said, turning painfully onto his side, this is getting me nowhere.

– We sleep now, she said. I exprane in the morning.

He fell asleep like a depleted log falling in a fireplace. In less than one minute he was alone in the dark, dreaming.

· 30 ·

The first day of spring.

The fire in the sky was over the equator and heading north. La Primavera.

He had been seeing a flower, here and there. But Romans still bundled up in sweaters and scarves, hats and overcoats. Furs. Boticelli would have frozen his ass this morning.

They had fixed his hotel room so that his ingenious manipulation of the thermostat, involving his nail clippers and his desk chair, produced no effect. The fan never came on. He was reminded in a counter-hemispheric way of his noisy but feckless air conditioner in Perth.

Fire has two phases. It is either leaping up with hunger, or expiring with satiety. The question is: how close to the fire do you want to be?

Just when he was wondering whether Eiko was something from his privileged dream, he heard her splash in the bathroom. Italian bathtubs are narrow, so that they will fill up fast. He had often wondered how one of those girthy Sicilian mamas could get into the bathtub, but then maybe they seldom did. No such problem with Eiko. He watched her half-float, yellow-white in the water.

– That'll cool that fire, he said.

– Not put it out, Harry, she said, smiling up at him, squinting to keep soap out of her eyes.

45

– How come you can say Harry but you cant say explain?

– I can exprane that, she said. I'm from Seattle.

– That expranes how you can say Harry, but it does not exprane, explain, why you cant say explain.

– But it makes me a mystery. Come into the bath, Harry.

– I think I am dreaming you, he said. The bathtub is too narrow.

– It make me narrow, too, yank.

She put on a licentious look, as best she could with the Asiatic equipment of her face.

– I said I'm not a Yank.

– I mean yank down those underwear and get in this tub. It's warm.

That persuaded him. He yanked and got in, or rather on. It didnt look very hopeful about getting in. But he had heard all the G.I. stories, and she wasnt from Seattle.

Later, on the rug in the other room, he asked about the intelligence-gathering she was going to explain.

– Still morning, Harry. Take me to the Via Venetto for coffee and cornetto.

No, he did not make the obvious crack, or rather remark. He sighed, and reached for their black leather jackets.

· 31 ·

The number 36 bus down Nomentana was crowded.

They had to force their way up the steps, and then stood in a tight packed crowd all the way down to the Termini at Piazza Cinquecento. As the bus swayed in and out of the first parking stalls, her body swung against him, and he felt the fire again. It was like the red molten earth in its last encounter with the white molten sun. It was like a quick wet steak on a hot griddle. The third time he felt the backs of her fingers on his risen aching, and the fourth time the swift grip of her fingers. He thought, that is, that they must have been hers. All the while her face was placid Asia. When her touch was not there the next time the fire was only worse.

He looked for her and saw that she was swaying half way up the bus, near the exit doors. Still placid, not much shorter than the Italian men.

Then she was in the crowd near the front. He moved as best he could past the overcoats and leather jackets, a rude North American, till he got his cumbersome body near the exit doors. The fire had subsided but not disappeared. It rose and fell a little as he watched her now, swaying with an old man with long white hair and a flat-brimmed black hat.

Then they were at the station, and the invigorated crowd poured out all the doors. He found her standing in front of a home-made sign that warned people about the Soviet source of the International Drug Epidemic. He stood beside her and put his hand on her buttock. She wiggled it off.

– Dont be rude, Harry.

– Are you saying rude, or lewd?

– Dont be funny, Harry.

They were walking inside the enormous cold train station.

– When I introduced myself to you, I just said that I was a lonesome traveller, he said. I never told you my name was Harry.

– Your name *is* Harry. Get two tickets for the Metro, Harry.

– Yes, but –

– Hurry.

They got off at the Barberini stop, and started walking up the neon snake of the Via Venetto.

– Look what I have, Harry.

Her little hands were full of wallets and pads of lire in money clips. The street was full of police with white holsters hanging in front of their crotches.

– Put that away, he said.

He hustled her into the first sit-down place they came to.

– We're rich, Harry.

– You were picking pockets on that bus, he said. I thought you were just exchanging fires, I mean feels.

– We have money to burn, yank.

– I told you –

– Yank a chair out for your date. I want a nice big breakfast. A bottle of Kav 1901 and an artichoke omerette.

· 32 ·

Now they stood in front of the Trevi fountain, where homely Italian schoolgirls were taking snapshots of each other, tall blond men with soft-soled shoes were examining bright streetmaps, unfolded as little as possible, and Gypsy women in multicoloured skirts were carrying one child each, practicing their grimaces of misery, fingers plucking the tweed jackets that went by.

Eiko threw a ten-thousand-lire note into the fountain, where it bobbed around on the never-settled surface. Neither the great alabaster figures nor the Italian idlers paid it any notice.

– A coin, he said. You're supposed to chuck in a coin.

– I wanted to make really sure I will return, she countered.

– Do I get my explanation, now that you are fed and assured another trip to Rome?

– Is the pope Italian?

– I know, does the dog shit on the sidewalk? Talk, Tokyo Rose, or I will throw *you* into the fountain.

– They did that in a movie, she said.

– But not in the late winter, he replied.

It was beginning to drizzle.

– All right, I begin to exprane, she said.

He wished they had brought an umbrella. But he was prepared to get wet if he could find out what was happening in the meantime.

– First there was fire, she said.

– Yes, I enjoyed that.

– Then the fire became the sea.

– This fountain?

He saw a man lean over the rail and pick up the banknote. Then he saw him reading it.

–Then half the sea became the earth, she continued, her hand touching him again.

The man put the banknote into his shirt pocket and looked over at them.

–The other half became thunder and lightning, she said loudly in his ear, and she grabbed his half-risen whatsit.

He turned his head to look at the man, who was now getting onto a motor scooter. He wanted to recognize him. All he could pick out of the ordinary was the sideburns. They were like those on a man in small-town Vancouver Island, lower than the hair level.

– Dont yank, he told her.

· 33 ·

Vancouver Island.

It is the top of a mountain, really, the valley between it and the mainland under salt water. So with the peninsula of Italy, really a chain of volcanic mountains rising above the clouds, particularly wet clouds, water in fact.

He was daydreaming while they walked up and down past the expensive shops that offered clothes with people's names on them between the Via del Corso and the Spanish steps. She had all her pockets filled with lire and quite a few deutschmarks, and she wanted to convert them, she said, into reality.

So fire cools and is converted into earth and sea. Every second for millions of years the earth has been crumbling,

49

flowing, falling, exploding into the sea, and every second for millions of years the creatures of the sea have been cast onto the shore to become earth for the passing feet of littoral lovers.

Ocean, with his horses, rose solid out of the Trevi water, not deigning to notice the coins people were tossing into the water. They were not seeking metamorphosis but only a vain repetition.

He knew you cant come back to Rome. You cant even visit the same little town on Vancouver Island twice.

She came out of a store with a gold lettered name on the wall over the front door, and she was transformed.

He didnt even remember what she had been wearing when she had gone in, something brown. Now she looked like a large tropical fish. The colours shifted as she moved. The silk blouse, all purples and greens, flashed away from her breasts as she spun in the street. A passing Italian man in a fur-collared overcoat walked hard into a chestnut brazier, scattering it and its contents noisily all over the cobbles.

The sun came out from behind a cloud and decanted light all over the walls and windows.

He took her hands and lifted them away from her sides. What a lucky man he was. He had the most amazing woman on the street, and she was going to tell him secrets he yearned to know.

– Let's go, Harry, she said, striding purposefully toward the Trinita dei Monti.

– Where?

– To the American hotels. I'm going to ride the elevators and make enough money for a little fur stole for my shoulders.

He felt like a fish out of water.

She seemed to be able to survive in any element you could throw at her.

Put her in a designer dress and sandals, and men in fancy hotel lobbies thud into one another uttering their *buon giornos*. Scatter her hair and slip her a pair of patched jeans, and she's the infant doyen of the demi-monde. He tagged along.

– You wait in the bar, Harry. I wont be long.

This is ridiculous and unnecessary, he wanted to say, in any language, but she was gone – there she was smiling a thank-you simper as three porcine midwest savings-and-loan fellows bared their teeth on the way into the elevator, impressing each other with their local ceremoniousness.

– *Prengo,* said one.

He was bowing and gesturing with a hand chubby enough for the gold wedding band to be overlapped by pink flesh, shafts of red hair on the backs of the fingers.

There, he thought, as he ambled indeed toward the bar, goes the death of some good Kansas earth.

Luckily it was an American sit-down bar, luckily first because he had to wait for a good while, and second because he was, for the first time since his travels had begun, drinking whiskeys, and after a few of those he found it not worthwhile to try sitting up straight.

He saw her walking by the street window, laughing and talking with two naval officers. They were headed toward the giantific U.S. embassy, a palace overlooking the Via Venetto and the Piazza Barberini. There goes the sea, he thought, and good riddance. He ordered another Glen Lewis whiskey and a bottle of Nastro Azzuro beer beside it.

Maybe he had seen the last of her. Good riddance. Maybe if he got good and drunk he could forget all this and go home tomorrow. Where was this home?

There was the English short story writer standing at the bar, having a cup of tea.

He got up, banging his thigh against the corner of his black table, but when he got there the woman was just a comparatively dowdy Italian woman of a certain age. Probably an Italian short story writer.

Maybe, he thought, the English short story writer was no more real than that. Maybe he'd been drunk for two months and just now was realizing it.

Maybe the sky was falling, too.

· 35 ·

There was the sensation of moving, and once in a while when he woke for a few seconds there was movement, yes.

It went on for hours. Or minutes that seemed like hours. He could not get entirely into his dreams because he was not alone.

And his neck was getting sore, bent as it was in what was probably the back seat of a car.

He woke when the sky was filled with light. It was lightning, flashes in the sky they were following, whoever they were. He was perhaps a part of they, them.

They followed, after days, or hours that seemed like days, the lightning, up a road up a mountain the car, it was perhaps a Volkswagen with the radio on, laboured slightly for, and a back of a head, a beautiful woman, showed with flashes of lightning behind it, or really in front of it.

Rain or was it pain slid down the window, and then he seemed to be in a bed.

· 36 ·

He woke to sunshine all around him, yet he was indeed in bed, in a double bed with brass posts.

The other side of the bed was wrinkled and turned down, and the bright light was all around him.

He saw then that he was surrounded by white walls, and in one wall the little window was open, where light poured in. He got up, his head sliced in half horizontally, and walked on bare feet over cool tiles to the window. The shutters were red, the curtain was white lace and fluttered into the room.

He looked out the window as if he were a character in a conventional U.S. short story, and received the full force of the bright sun in his eyes, which were cut in half horizontally, but at least he could see now, and he saw that he was looking from a cliff down over grey-green fields of olive trees toward a wide expanse, he had to call it, of blue sea with a light mist over it.

If he was still in Italy rather than Greece or Spain, and if it was morning, this was the Adriatic coast, south. If it was evening it must be the other coast. But he had seen the Adriatic before, and it had had just such a mist over it.

Or was he in Albania? Is that what this was all about?

– There is a new sun every day.

So said her voice behind him, with a put-on Japanese accent.

He turned carefully and looked. She was wearing white slacks, white shirt, white sandals, and a white fur around her shoulders.

– Ah, he said, Miss Rising Sun.

–Herself, she said. Do you feel up to some caffe latte and pannini? There is a darling little restaurant just a few steps up the street. I can even fetch a tray from them.

–Where the hell, he said, if you dont mind my Anglo-Saxon brusqueness, am I?

– We, she said. Us.

–Okay.

– We are in the medieval quarter of Ostuni.

– Great. Where is Ostuni?

– In the olive, wine, and cheese section of Puglia.

– Puglia.

– You'll love it.

– I'm going to have your ass, he said, stepping across the wonderful tile floor.

– All right, she said. Then coffee.

· 37 ·

The streets of Ostuni were winding and narrow, and sometimes they had a few steps in them.

The exterior walls, too, were whitewashed, but the concept of exteriority didnt seem apt here – the surface of the street was so clean that it seemed like a floor. There were no sidewalks, the street meeting the wall flush, as in a hallway. In fact the streets were often no wider than a sidewalk, and women were to be seen whitewashing, sweeping with besoms, or talking from windows. There were no men – they would be seen later in the regular part of the town, hanging around in small groups at the main piazza.

Eiko walked a little in front of him, leading the way around intriguing white corners, silently pointing out a vista. In the narrowest defiles he could feel the cool emanating from the ancient stones though the spring-at-last sun was high. In the narrowest of the narrow the sun found only a pathway between shadows, and thus it was only as wide as a man's foot is long.

They went into the medieval cathedral and came back out, from dark cool to white cool.

– How do you like your new home, asked the white-clad Oriental.

– It is, he replied, the most charming place I have ever been in the world.

– Good, she said. I knew you would like it as much as I do.

– They told you I would, did they?

– They?

She was leaning against a low wall with her back to the Albanian sea. He thought about pushing her over and running to hide in Stockholm.

– They. The people who are recruiting me or leading me to a perverse end.

He kept his hands in the pockets of his rumpled cotton slacks.

– You can forget a perverse end, she said. They are indeed recruiting you. Have you read any interesting short stories lately?

– You mean here, of course?

– Of course.

– You mean the book that was on my bedside table and which I purchased in the bookshop at Heathrow airport?

– Yes, of course, that one.

– Yes. It is a series of short stories concerned with women athletes. A fresh subject, I thought. Are we at last beginning to talk about things?

– Yes, we are, said Eiko. Would you care to step into the shadow?

· 38 ·

– Did you notice anything peculiar about that collection of short stories, asked the white rose of the east.

They were walking in front of the medieval cathedral, slowly, ambling, like Italians. They were two unemployed people in an undreamt land.

– Well, he said.

He was unused to being asked a literary opinion. It was like writing a book, every day writing a little section of a book, in foreign cities, a book carried in a small suitcase; especially it was like seeing that it was there in the afternoon, having forgotten that it was time to write in the book, and

55

then going to one's room and beginning to write, perhaps with a piece of dialogue, a question, let us say. It was like that, this position he was now in, but he did not know that. He was not a writer of books or even of a book, certainly not a book about someone he referred to as 'he,' who was trying to find out how to live in pre-Socratic metonymy. He knew no such words.

–Well, he said, you mean something aside from the unusual subject, the female athletes?

– Yes, something.

They walked again where they had been walking, she as white as the walls, he as rumpled as the sea.

–I am, he said, not qualified as an interrogator, is that what you say?

– Critic, she said.

–I am not qualified as a critic of literature, but I thought that the collection of stories was a little, uneven.

She went into the little tabaccheria on the corner and bought a package called Kim. He did not Stop. She ran to catch up, one hand holding cigarettes, the other clutching her wrap.

–Was it as if the first few stories were written by one person, and the rest by someone else?

– I suppose so, yes.

– By a number of other people, perhaps?

– Sure.

– Did those latter, multi-authored stories –

– *Perhaps* multi-authored, he said.

– Okay, Yank. Did those latter stories seem inferior?

– What do you want me to yank?

–We'll get to that later, Harry. Did they seem to you to be inferior?

–All right, he said. We will agree that the latter stories, perhaps the last sixty-five percent of the book, seem to have been done by someone other than the titular author –

—I like that, it's confusing. Authorized title would be clearer, but would mean something far less interesting.

She was smoking and walking and gesticulating and checking out the underclothes on all the strings hanging in the sun between windows. On one line hung a puppet of a female figure, dressed like a miniature woman of the region, in multi-coloured patterns.

– Hmm, she said, indicating it with her head.

– Hmm, he responded. And we agree that the latter stories are inferior, in a literary way. So?

She stopped walking, but spoke without turning to look at him.

–If there were no sun, she said, not all the stars in the heavens could prevent the coming of the night.

· 39 ·

They were picking at their first plate in the white hostaria around the corner from 'their' house.

Little octopus legs, rings of squid, curled shrimp, bits of greenish stuff, some kind of winkle or baby clam. Olive oil, lemon. It was delicious, Adriatic, could go on forever if you picked one little bit at a time. Mysterious life from the sea, cousins offshore from Albania.

She was still speaking in koans.

–Morning, she said, is distinguished from night by the Bear. Please try some of this Locorotondo. It is bottled a few kilometers from here, a blend of two local whites.

He drank some of the local pride. It was serviceable, not as good as the whites of Western Australia.

–I am not a follower of the horoscope, he said, spearing a tentacle.

–Opposite the Bear is the path of fire-trailing Zeus, she continued.

He poured a little mineral water into his wine.

– Are we now discussing godless communism, he asked.

She smiled a quick disappearing celestial smile.

– Let us remind ourselves, she almost whispered, that understanding is common to all mortal people, yet each of us acts as if his or her intelligence were personal or even private.

– I know what you mean, he said, flashing an occidental grin.

– That *is* clever, she allowed, and that is also fortunate if true, dago.

– Oh, now after a few weeks in this country, speaking enough words to get a coffee and a newspaper, I am mistaken for a dago?

Now she allowed impatience to cross her face, something non-Japanese people are seldom permitted to see.

– Day go by too fast for errors in understanding, she said.

– You do that on purpose, he said.

She lit a cigarette while waiting for the second plate. She had a habit of sticking her bottom lip out to one side and blowing smoke up past her little nose.

– There is another difference between the stories, she told him. The first ones are true, and the latter ones are all made up to conform with suggestions that came from an office. Let us say that the office is east of the publisher.

· 40 ·

He treated himself to a first-class ticket on the Rapido from Bari to Rome.

At first it wasnt very rapido, but by the time it sniffed the first smog lying along the Sacco River, it was quietly electric, downhill, fairly lifting off the tracks.

He saw the back sides of old brick buildings, grass growing on every horizontal surface. Grape vines in the late winter looked like columns of *crucificattos*. Monte Cassino was almost new, solid and square on its hilltop. Even the unbelievably sadly destroyed was somewhere in the southern sunlight.

Men were busy right now, cutting a line in the hard Renaissance wall up the stairs to San Pietro in Vincole, to install a wire for telephones. Italy was falling down, and aging men were building it again, making an accord with decay. RAI DUE is sending telemetric images of a scanty gown and black swimsuit into the air over the gummy plinths of the Roman Republic.

The most particular designs of men and women, the most beautiful perceived order in the cosmos, Michelangelo's marble vein down the biceps of Moses, the faint trace of the line from your warm prairie kitchen to the dock at Rhodes, they are a sweeping of random objects, trash gathered without meaning. The stars miss one another randomly.

Then why had he been led by a whiff of design to the Nipponese seminar on the Puglian hilltop? And why was he obeying the second command to go home? Why, especially, had they chosen him, an ordinary Harry with no literary ambition, to correct an edition of short fictions?

Also, why should he risk a mittel European dungeon or many steel bullets just because a crazed association of international bibliophiles had chosen him, apparently at random?

They were awfully schematic in their randomness, and they were uneconomical, inefficient in their scheming.

Still, he had advanced, he thought, a step, the width of the sun, toward understanding.

· 41 ·

Heathrow airport was, as always, cruelly overheated.

It was probably in propitiation of wealthy Arabs. He felt as if he were a beast of burden, forced to carry leather weights on his shoulders, to plod the long glass corridors, whiffing the bad gasses.

He felt like an edible animal, driven from the field into the pens.

He sat down to drink a miserable British coffee, already hankering for a Roman bar. He sat down for one minute, until the loud hard human voice impelled him on again, deeper into the pens.

4 · A Going Concern

Consciousness, he decided, is how it is composed.

While his travelled clothes snarled in the washer he sat next door to the laundromat, in a Chinese burger place he remembered as decrepit twenty-five years ago.

Consciousness is how it is composed: he had travelled across three continents looking for it, and he had been riding it all along. Wherever he went, the boundaries of consciousness were out of reasonable sight, beyond bespectacled imagination, and its consular roads were marked out by his travelling. Now he was at home.

–This means, he said to a nicotine cowboy at the next ancient formica table top, that your soul is not shrunken inside you, it is all around, and other people feel free to walk through it.

–Far fucking out, said the other, his old army jacket wet on the shoulders. He had been sitting in this place twenty-five years ago.

–It extends deep beyond comprehension in every direction, he said.

– You're right on there, said his neighbour.

–Substance and activity are the same thing when it comes to soul, he persisted.

– Soul. Fuckin' A, said the nicotine man.

61

– Or psyche, if you prefer that term.

–I been psyched by the best of them, said the man. The best and the worst of them, too.

– Or self. Some would prefer that simple word.

– Dont know if I still have one of those, said the man.

Then he spotted a long cigarette butt just left by a woman who was heading for the cash register, and leaped over to get it.

–Souls form communities, and one's growing awareness of self is in some fundamental mysterious but necessary way bound up with a growing recognition of other centres of awareness. You cant make a wheel without spokes.

–I gotta go now, said the man, but he didnt move in his ramshackle aluminum chair.

By now the stuff would be ready for the dryer. He would maneouver for the right change when he paid for his, and his neighbour's coffee.

· 43 ·

Now he was home for keeps, and enjoying the chance to wear his stupid old clothes and sneakers, go through the day with dirty hair, eat whatever was still its original colour in the refrigerator.

Sitting on his balcony, watching the people below scuttling in the rain, he was nearly content. His soul was nearly at rest, nearly peaceful. He felt the way an author does when he takes a day off from his book, but he didnt know that.

Of course that nearly was nearly everything. Because his knowledgeable mind knew that the idea of his, or a my, was not truly supportable. When he looked at the mist in the air over the sea, he knew that his eyeballs could be turned inward.

Whatever the peaceful soul or the rested psyche was, it was a vapour that went around the world like an ocean in the air. He had learned that much. The part of 'his' soul that was not easy was murmuring some sort of plot in Europe or Australia right now.

Well, he had decided that he was not going to have any more to do with this short story escapade. They could get another editor, use schematic chance again.

Now his psyche, at least, was not at rest. Whatever the soul or the self even was, it was too vapourous to be contained. It was probably the base material of everything else, and it was so ephemeral as to be a great escaper. His body might become an empty envelope on the balcony.

Damn those women, anyway.

If they phoned he would hang up. If one spoke to him in a restaurant he would stuff food in his mouth and read a day-old newspaper.

He was going to sit still.

But his soul was restless. He could feel it moving around right now. And everything else. If he was ever to know anything he could only know it while it was moving. Twisting.

He tried to sit still on the balcony. He could feel nervous jumping like particles of mist inside his head. What does the cat do when it is time to sit still?

He licks.

That goes double for me, he thought.

· 44 ·

He felt as if he were becoming a philosopher.

Sitting on a log at Kitsilano Beach, looking at the ocean, a light grey, like the cover of Fodor's guide to Germany.

No, he felt like somebody's example in a book of philosophical enquiry.

63

One gull stood on a sheet of smooth wet sand, moving its tail.

No, philosophical opinion.

On a dry hot day in Western Australia he could go for hours thinking of nothing but his skin and perhaps what his skin was closest to. But Vancouver was a dense bog of soul. Everything was moist. When the plane had broken through the lowest layer of cloud and come in slowly over the green Richmond flats, he had seen squares of water that were supposed to be plots of truck garden vegetables. Looked like rice fields, or no, fish hatcheries.

But twisting and moving, yes, he felt sometimes now as if he were an unwilling character in a philosophical narrative, the sort of thing he would never read. His ex-wife had tried for a year during their wet courtship to get him to read the novels of Jean-Paul Sartre. They were so boring. Nobody ever moved in them.

People always said that all this April rain was what made this the evergreen playground. Mothers sent their toddlers out to play in the rain, yellow slickers with red STOP signs on them, or the latest cartoon animal, a grinning cat, a winsome skunk.

Rain puts food on your table, boy.

I guess, he thought as he got up to walk across the wet grass and homeward, this damp makes for soul. Psyche, as they call it, starts here, takes to the air and drifts eastward. Well, he would not. When the time came, they could look for another soul to buy. They had been rather vague on a price, anyway. Anyway?

How do you, he thought, grow a soul?

He was sitting in Section 52, Row EE, Seat 101, at the Dome, watching a desultory game between the Seattle Mariners and the Toronto Blue Jays. The names of the cities and teams would have seemed a joke to him in 1948, when he was a knowledgeable baseball fan. Tautology.

A tight infield, had there been one here, would have taught him. Baseball honours the individual.

It was Easter Sunday.

But it depends totally on unnegotiated balletic cooperation of the ensemble. The mind seems shared. The heart is alone. The brain tries alone to understand language. But the mind is language moving where more than one is, moving.

He could hardly sit still in Section 52, his unlucky number. The ceiling was made of arching cloth. The floor was made of durable fabric. The rest was concrete and plastic. The usual sounds of a game were withheld from the small throng, like a shoe dropped during a wave-burst.

There seemed little opportunity for soul in such a place. The ballplayers tried, making their usual movements, but it was as if they were doing it in another dimension, viewed through an electronic scope.

Terrible. The game was indoors and the attendants were Canadian. It was like eating a hamburger made in England.

The soul, he was just thinking, grows according to its own laws, and cannot be copied from television onto real estate, when he saw someone buying a frosted malt in Section 54.

It was the woman from the Thai restaurant, in Toronto, in Seattle.

The light rain does fall, the light mist does rise, soul clap he hands, and the fire that sproings from thee lives on the death of air, that may not be right but that's what happens in a closet of wet steel, you're locked in a dying, mister.

Too much rain on the pate, any man would go nuts, punch the next toddler he sees, kick a cat off a dead bird, walk into traffic before it has a chance to slow down, much less halt.

This rain might bring the flowers that bloom in May and the spirit that loves the earth beyond reasonable regard, but it is bad for the gabardine slacks.

Who goes there? Who is that flitting from awning to awning on West Fourth Avenue where the candle-sellers got poor before they took tai-chi and got familied and moved to the residentials? Could have been an ork phantom, a soul heading to its station, probably the woman from the Thai restaurant in Toronto, not the one that won a prize.

He had not thought much about soul, or better soul-stuff since he was a warm weather Christian child in a town whose name meant the meeting of the waters. He had been brought up in a fond desert valley, decent as the cowslips, is that what they were, along the couchgrass hills. Soul there was no shifty streetcorner mugger out to protect civilization as we know it.

Soul, once it gets dry, is wise and good. Maybe he ought to get home, move in with his own Mémère, be good. It was all he wanted, a child, in them days.

Here he could get fresh bagels and architecture magazines, but it rained all the time, gave birth to souls, all skulky.

And they wanted him to go back to soaking Europe, under the avalanche of the deepest winter since 1956.

All his soul wanted right now was to get as wet as it could.

It urged him to sit in the beer parlour at the Waldorf Hotel and pour the suspect draft dark into his face hole, wherefrom it would descend like winter down a tube inside where some people, when they are not attentive to their surround, think the soul is a poor captive.

Wet wet, more wet.

– More beer, he said.

He was not sitting with friends, but he knew the people at a nearby table. The table was round-topped, and had a worn terrycloth cover affixed with elastic underneath. As hard as he looked he could not tell what colour it was. It was some colour. It was not, that is, devoid of colour. A kind of light colour, maybe a dirty fuzzy pastel of some sort.

Detail is important. Some people, getting wet, dont care about details – they are on vacation from details. Others fix on details, at least for a while. The brand name on a bent cigarette butt.

It would not have to be called a colour. More wet, said the soul.

It was as if his soul wanted to drink itself to death. That way, he would not have to get into yet another jumbo jet and fly back over the Arctic.

But of course he did.

This time in a DC-10, how he hated that airplane, partly because of its reputation as a crasher. Now someone had opined that it was preferable to fly in a DC-10 over anything else because no airplane could have been gone over more minutely than this one, since the well-photographed disasters. Gone over in detail. But twelve or thirteen thousand meters over Iceland, he had thought that that argument simply does not hold up (oh brush something like wood-work) – that one's experience says that once some product, as they say, fails at its bidden task, so it will often fail, no matter how we try to patch it up because it was so expensive.

Jet-lagged once more, he tried to collect his thoughts, and his bedraggled luggage. Here he was, then, not on Alten-steinstrasse, but on Garystrasse, and who the hell was Gary. His head stuffed with ill-fitting old rags made from historical socks. He had followed instructions, and here he was in a large blond-wood apartment all alone with his wrinkled clothes. This was not intrigue at all. It was foolishness, not worth thinking about, or rather, thinking about it would yield no satisfactory order, no enticing chaos.

When he and his overly-wet soul had walked or lurched out the side door of the Waldorf beer parlour a few nights ago, they had been met on the sidewalk by a young boy. Luckily, because without the guidance of the young boy, he and his soul might have walked blindly till they came to a downhill grade, and then fallen to the bottom. Unluckily, because the boy was not his son and did not take him home.

He arrived home the next day, where the young boy helped him pack his bags, inexpertly to be sure. And now here he was. When the plane broke through the last layer of dark clouds, he had seen the Wall. From the air it looked thin.

· 49 ·

The rain was still following him around the crust of the earth.

He was carrying his Roman umbrella with him all day on his long neighbourhood walks, past the large monopoly board houses, wondering whether these were more than thirty-five years old, hearing nevertheless jet fighters up above and wondering about that. The island of West Berlin has an air space that can be crossed in seconds, and who was doing that? Never mind.

American soldiers in steel helmets on Clayallee. Never mind that. Have another Winston cigarette, dont let the Red Army Faction cyclist see the bright package. Forget that.

Rain so much, so often, so persistently, he would get wet clear through to the soul; no, the soul is all about, and it is damp already. There had better be some sunshine soon or poor old soul will become water itself, and flow away, into a Berlin storm drain. Little pun there, better than the ones you will suffer in a redhead's novel. He should have stayed in her Vancouver, where the rain rains and the souls soul.

His feet hurt and his head could not figure it out: psyche is born of the wet but dies by drowning. He who lives by the deluge shall die by the deluge. Nothing comes after that.

He wondered whether it was raining in East Berlin, where the short stories were so inexpertly written.

He felt as if he could begin to think straight if he could only find some dry ground to stand on. A bit of ground could put the muddle of water behind him, liberate him from noxious insects that breed in swamps, allow him to forget his horizontal origin in the mire.

But water springs out of the soil, too. He was a lot better off in Western Australia, where the water is the flat blue ocean and the earth is the hard dry crib of the gum trees. There he did some thinking. But there he went off with a sailor away from home from the sea.

—Mud'll make you do a lot of low conjecture, he said aloud to the slightly echoing apartment. Tomorrow the sun'll shine, and they will have to make contact with a clear-thinking man.

Everywhere he went lately people would ask him are you writing something now, and he would say no, I am not a writer, you have mistaken me for someone else.

After a while he thought perhaps yes I should say I am working on a book that will remain as fragments for restless readers many centuries from now. I will fill it with contradictions and they will observe how poetically they are expressed, and call them paradoxes. What is it about, they will say, and I will say that it is an adventure intrigue set in all the foreign places I have been running around to.

They will say your writing resembles that of a well-known English short story writer.

But he was not a writer.

When he admired the blue-eyed German women he was not admiring them as a writer would.

He got up when the second alarm clock went off. In his sleep he had been startled, thinking it was the telephone. In the apartment there was a green-and-white-swirly plastic telephone that he or someone was paying for, but no one had phoned during his three nights there.

He let the lukewarm water with its thin shards of Berlin rust run into the narrow European tub while he shaved his chin and neck. Then he sat in the tub with the water up to his hipbone, and closed his eyes again until the water got cold.

On TV the East Berliners were showing nuthatches and tadpoles.

He went by them into the kitchen and opened the low refrigerator, stepping back to look inside as if he did not know what was in there. A bottle of orange juice was in there. It had separated, dark thick stuff at the bottom, light thin fluid at the top, unseen high-heeled shoes clicking by on the sidewalk below. He shook.

They'd told him to keep walking, to go out every day and walk.

When the 'time was right' they would tell him what he was doing here, or rather what he would be doing there.

He kept getting what he wanted, a little at a time, and each time he did, it cost him a little soul. He thought about that when he read that Berlin is situated in the great midcontinent bog. Werent they always finding perfectly preserved bodies of people from the semihistorical past in the bogs? Perfect bodies, old, new, but no soul. All leaked out into the damp earth.

For three or four (four?) days he had stayed in the neighbourhood, broadly defined, doing a lot of walking, but all of it in Dahlem. All he saw were U.S. soldiers and Berlin university students. The soldiers wore green uniform fatigues and high black boots with lines across the toes. They could have been 1960 U.S. soldiers. They stood in pairs in front of the officers' club, and came to attention with their weapons whenever anyone went between them, through the door, on the way to American corn whiskey and dinner. Turkish cleaning women with kerchiefs on their heads and cheap knitted stockings on their bowed legs scuttled out the back door and gabbled in their angry-sounding language as they moved in a constantly re-tied knot on their way to the bus stop.

It is hard to resist the call of the heart's desire. He saw their husbands walking with portable stereos next day through the Tiergarten. They carried their souls, and these were heavy on their arms.

The students were older than students in other countries because university is free, and subsidies are paid, and unemployment is high. People were always telling you that.

71

He finally went to Zehlendorf to report to police on Konigstrasse. They wanted to tell their computers what his religion was, and what his mother's name was. On the way to the police station he thought he saw a naked woman sitting in a deck chair on a balcony at eye level, but he was looking through a line of cedar trees that might become a hedge in time, and then he was at the police station.

But he walked more slowly and looked more carefully on the way back, and yes, there she was, now lying down in the spring morning sunshine. She was on her back, but turned a little to one side. One perfect pyramid of skin pointed straight up. He felt impulsive desire.

· 53 ·

The young naked woman on Berlin television had exactly the same body as the young naked woman on Rome television.

The little black birds near the Brandenburg Gate probably flew back and forth over the wall. He had not seen any doing so, however.

Those were things that passed before his eyes, and remained with the old rags in his head. *Lumpen.* He did not really want anything he saw. He wanted Annalise. That is, why not? She appeared one day and one night in Rome. She could appear among the new stone streets of Berlin, why not? She had left him a note on a small square of paper, and a poor little fellow sore and red from the all-night night. Why not?

– Yah, why not?

So said the middle-aged Kraut he was drinking with, *rotwein*, was it? Lots of it. Before they had got really drunk, before the man had become a mound of spillings, shirt out of pants, a corner here, a corner there, bare belly looking through where buttons were undone or gone, straight sweated-in hair hanging over an ear, grey striped woolen sock down over black shoe with *currywurst* sauce on it, he had said the last words that had made good sense in their Anglo-Teutonic discussion.

–If we could all have our wishes come true and our desires fulfilled, my friend, the condition of humankind would not be any better than it is right now.

Now he was only saying the German equivalent of those raspy-voiced repetitions about the school of hard knocks and Dieppe you hear from old stubbled guys in brown pants in awful beer parlours all over Canada.

And he himself was no better. He was what his Irish uncle who was not Irish always used to call 'desthroyed' by drink, and saying nothing at all intelligent.

– Do you know where Annalise is, he asked.

– *Nein,* no Annalise, I find you hippy girl.

–There are no more hip – only punkies now, they got nice hair but they think you think it's ugly.

–I get you hippy girl. Big hips, big ass, you say ass in your language, America?

The Kraut's tie was hanging down the back of his jacket.

– No America, Canada.

– Kan –

– Were you in Dieppe?

– What Dieppe, said the Kraut. I was born 1934 in Silesia.

He felt the rotting wine move when he shifted his ass on the cane chair. He was what his mother used to call ignorant. You are so ignorant, she would say when he dropped something.

– Are you a spy, too, he asked.

· 54 ·

There was no young boy to guide him home or anywhere else that night.

He finally got a taxi and fell into a private world before it

73

turned off the Ku'damm. Somehow, not knowing how he had paid the driver, he got into his apartment, and with all his clothes on, dropped on top of the eiderdown and disappeared from all human intelligence.

He woke when his portable Sony came on, some U.S. corporal reading the news. Canada's hopes for a berth in soccer's world cup playoffs rose as the Canadian team defeated Guatemala two to one, said the corporal, probably black.

Despite a head filled with broken bricks, he fluttered with excitement.

The U.S. president announced Saturday that the outcry in Europe and the United States would not change his mind about visiting the Nazi graveyard at Bitburg, said the NCO.

He trembled to hear it. But he often trembled when he had been drinking late the night before.

The voice inside the brushed aluminum continued, rather loudly.

South Africa is determined to ignore criticism from the United Nations and proceed with its plans for a provisional government in Namibia.

It was almost more than he could bear. Shivering with excitement or something, he got up to attend to the radio. Draining its batteries.

An international delegation of artists and authors will visit their counterparts in East Berlin next week, said the young man.

Hardly able to control his shaking, he pushed the off button.

Were those items really in that order? Sports first?

He felt like a fool, sitting on his bed in yesterday's clothes. Time was not the essence. You cannot step into the same trousers twice. His pantlegs were spirals of cloth around his legs. Standing to straighten them, he put his hands into his pockets, his risen head feeling like a Gothic church bell.

He felt a wad of paper in his right hand pocket. When he took it out, he dropped thousands and thousands of Deutschmarks onto the parquet floor.

· 55 ·

He was a fool, or he had been a fool for some time.

Words had been appearing to him so often, so continually, as large painted letters, neon lights, whatever those plastic lights are, words he had to read rather than just notice, Italian words, German words, too long, with marks over the letters, Deutschmarks on the bed, he remembered the marks on her chest, no, and even Australian words, what did they mean, exactly, when the Australians write 'timber' they mean the boards you buy at a store. Killed on the premises.

A fool, or let us say as his friend Guy used to couch it, stupid. Stupid. It means able to hear but deaf all the same. Means nobody home though they are standing right there all the time. The boatload of the stupid, let us say, the DC-10 full of the stupid. Maybe one man is reading Lucretius, but the rest believe that wisdom is for someone else to bother with, perception is for the busy and the ambitious.

His name should have been Luke rather than Harry.

Maybe he should go right back to bed, among all the dirty marks, no, they were brand new except for thin little creases from his tortured pocket.

Fool, because getting tired of words, he quit reading them, and getting drunk on schnapps he quit hearing them.

One of them was Silesia. The year was interesting, too. 1948, say, take away 1934 leaves fourteen. His history could use a little polish, it's true, but he remembered his own fifteenth year. That year his father was also his history teacher; there was a lot of continuity to his life that year.

That was the year a lot of German DP's started showing up in his home town. A few years later you were not supposed to say DP, even if you were talking about a double play. Just in case. It had become a shameful word, like 'coon,' or 'breed.'

The alarm clock went off, because he had set it for fifteen minutes after the radio.

But surely he didnt stay awake long enough to wind it last night?

· 56 ·

—Get your clothes on, Stupid, and come to the eating room, yes?

Kitchen. Voice in the apartment. Think.

—I am this morning making for you some breakfast, like a good *hausfrau*.

Of course it was Annalise, his favourite DP. Her crinkled blonde hair hung over one of her deep-set blue eyes. She wore no discernible makeup, but her face was shining and so was the sun through the white scrims. He had not thought of lowering the shutters the night before, not thought even of removing his tight blue socks.

She was spooning coffee into the filter. Her fingers were long and narrow with square ends, and he remembered how they could wrap, how her knuckles too could rap a sign for her desire. She was, now that she was standing, nearly six feet tall, wonderful. His favourite DP.

— My favourite DP, he said.

His voice sounded like a coal chute heard through a floor. Therefore, either his throat or his ear was in bad shape this morning.

— What is this, DP, she asked.

—Displaced person. That's what we called you mittel Europeans when you came with your headscarves over to our place after the war.

—I was born in Berlin ten years after the war, and here I am still, she said. You do not look so well. I think you made perhaps a fool of yourself last night.

—DP, he said. I cant help thinking of Germans as DP's. Nazis or DP's. I know all about Volkswagen and Häagen-Dazs, and those expensive eyeglasses that start with R, and the economic miracle, and your beautiful long tubular legs and white ankle socks, but you'll always be my favourite DP.

—I think, do you mind, I think you might be a *blind-glaubige*, she said.

— A blind believer? What?

— No, a bigot, you say.

—Yaw, yaw, he said. I have a sacred belief in what I see. I am a religious man, oh yaw. And I just cant help thinking of you as a DP. When we next go to bed, if we ever do, and why not, I seem to be a rich man, I am going to think of you as a poor little DP, a six-foot little DP.

—Have some coffee, Stupid, she said. No body is going to bed now. It is a beautiful sunny Berlin afternoon.

— Morning?

— Afternoon.

—Even, he said, on Altensteinstrasse, I suppose. Why did my instructions say Garystrasse?

—In case you left little pieces of paper in rumpled hotel rooms, she said.

· 57 ·

They were walking together through the Grunewald, surrounded by many varieties of family dogs, which were, because it was Sunday, dashing among the trees and up and down the paths, sniffing each other's fundaments.

Families strolled down the wide paths, carrying dog leashes. Nazi widows sat on every park bench. Slightly younger people were slowly riding bicycles laden with devices. The sun shone, trying to warm up spring in the

77

northern interior of the cultural continent. In every direction there were nuclear-tipped rockets sitting heavy on their silent propellants.

– Are you a good friend of Lotus Blossom, the dip, he enquired.

He saw that she, like many of the other Berlin women, was carrying a long twig and sometimes trailing it in the dust.

– You mean Eiko, I presume, she said. No, not a good friend, but a good sister.

– In the organization.

– In the organization, yes. As you said this afternoon, on the editorial board. Are *you* a good friend of Eiko?

– We did get along at times, before I left her in the heel of the boot.

– Did she make your job clear to you?

– One of them, yes. The other, presumably the one you are interested in, well, maybe not quite. I keep thinking that I am gathering more information, have to be, given my modestly capable intelligence, but I dont know more than I do.

She smiled an achingly beautiful German smile, and took his arm, her German breast pushed against his biceps, and he was carrying his tweed jacket over his other arm.

– Most people, she said, dont really know what is happening to them, or around them. But they think they do, yes? You are really not a fool, just your usual, well, man.

– Thank you. You are not your usual woman.

– Thank you. Did Eiko tell you to expect a contact who would leave you some money and not expect a receipt?

– Uh huh, now that you mention it.

– Now you have the money, dont you? In case you did not count it when you took it off the bed and put it in that useless hiding place, there are six hundred thousand *Deutschmarks* in large bills. You will not declare the three hundred thousand you take across the frontier.

– We say border where I come from.

– We say frontier. Surely you receive a whiff of intrigue when you hear the word?

– Actually I get a whiff of currywurst, he said. My treat.

He deftly nipped into the line in front of the little stall, trying to keep out of the way of three urchins in short pants with insecure ice cream confections.

– Harry, she said.

– Yes, *mein klein liebling?*

– Make mine a *lange wiener mit Senf.*

· 58 ·

That night there was rain just beyond their reach, just past the terrace.

Downtown Berlin was said never to close down, but here in the comfortable residential zone of separate thirty-year-old houses, all the lights were off before 10:30 at night. So they did not see the rain, and because of the grass all around this apartment building in the little park, they could not hear it. They just knew it was there. Their bodies were hot with shoving each other, so they could not feel the cool of the rain in the air. Maybe they just smelled it there on the great Interior plain.

Of all the women this strange adventure had brought him to, the German was the most energetic, and she was strong, stronger than the Indian Ocean sailor. As soon as they kissed, her tongue was all around his mouth like a hungry awakened snake. Her body too could not take anything slowly, but twisted and plunged, thumped him till he had to writhe and jump to keep close. She would not let him rest, but threw him onto the floor, grabbed at his buttocks with her large hands. She bit him and wiped drool over his shoulder. His mouth was full of her crinkled hair. She had a long finger up his surprised anus. He put his tongue behind her ear and she

79

detonated, falling all over his person like seven naked children greeting their dad. When he lay on his back, desperate for a moment's recuperation, maybe a cigarette and a few words, she kneeled astride his face and rocked her pelvis, allowing him to take a wet breath of air every third swing.

−Christ, he said, an hour later, having been wakened from a minute's sleep, you are so demure, so Lutheran, such a cold northern beauty.

−I like to explore my faculties at large, she said, playing with his debilitated *wurst*. Unlike most people, including yourself, I want a hundred percent input from my senses.

−I think you have fucked me blind, he complained.

−You will need your eyes, she said. And you will need to keep in better touch with them. I do not believe you saw me at the Flughaven Tegel last week.

−I *had* just flown for eleven or twelve hours, he said. I was making my way through sensory deprivation and passport control.

−If you had smelled smoke, she said, you would have looked for fire. If everything were smoke, you would have to distinguish each thing by its smell.

−You smell wonderful, he said.

−Oh, you know the right thing to say.

She said that from her throat, and when she did the right thing with her eyelashes, a near miracle began to occur.

· 59 ·

All animals are sad after making love, or as animals call it, doing sex.

The gorgeous German lay asleep with her head on his breast, a line of sweet drool joining them, mouth-corner to nipple. A television announcer, or at least his cadences, could be heard rising from the apartment of the happy Japanese below.

80

He was sad, and for some reason unable to summon sleep to his sleepiness. That was heaven, this is heaven, she had said in Rome. But now they were in Berlin, and he could smell smoke. The smoke was other souls. In Hell people know each other by smoke alone.

The long woman smelled as if she had been burning. The only sound was the mumbling TV set below, and it sounded like the feckless beseeching of the gone, the going, the disappearing beyond succour. If he were to take a chance on waking her by sniffing deeply, he thought he would be able to smell a television set burning.

How many wraithes in this part of the continent had gone up to join the overcast?

Was he sleeping, was he dreaming this? No, he could see nothing in the dark, but he could smell her breath, with that something so many Germans have on their breath, something they eat in the morning. He could not imagine what it was. It was like smoke made of oil.

Was he really going to do what they wanted him to do, try to pick up the last piece in the short story puzzle? He had told Annalise that he wanted a solution to this whole mystery. Mysteries are not solved, she had said, you can write a whole book about a mystery and it remains a mystery.

Wont I know what this is all about when I finish, he had asked.

You will be an initiate, she had said. Initiates are wiser, she had said. Wise people are those who have gone deeper into the mystery. People who solve puzzles and then can distance themselves from them are merely smarter, she had said.

That's better than being dead, he had said.

If the mystery truly exists, then death does not, she had said.

Not able to sleep, he was itching for a cigarette, but he chose her sleep over smoke.

· 60 ·

Usually he didnt feel or hear the rumble of the U-Bahn from his bedroom any more.

The little yellow trains of the BVG's number 2 line went right by his apartment building, in a little defile between him and the U.S. military radio station he could see through the young trees with their half-opened leaves.

But a train must have gone by. An answering quiver went through her body, and if he had at last been asleep he no longer slept, and she twice tried to snuggle for more sleep on his chest, but then opened her deep-set blue eyes and smiled with them. His arm on that side was totally without sensation, a heap of weight belonging to itself.

– *Gut Morgen*, she said, her German voice made even more fetching by its waking-up croak.

– The hell it is, he said.

He indicated the bedside window, where for the second night in a row he had neglected to lower the shutter. The sky was dark and low, and the nearly bare thirty-year-old trees were whipping in the wind. They could not hear the rain, but they knew it was raining. At least it was not snowing.

– What a symbolic day for your first visit through the wall, she said, and jumped out of bed.

She was in the bathroom and had the water running into the narrow tub and was tinkling on the toilet before he got his feet onto the floor. His arm hung in front of him, a thick tube of foreign meat.

– I'm not going today, he shouted.

– Oh? Oh? she shouted back. But we have a window today.

– I know all about that. But I am not going over there until I have a nice day to do it.

He went into the bathroom and rubbed the green bar of soap on her freckled back.

– The circumstances, she said, not failing to lean her head forward and hold her bushy hair up to enjoy his soapy hands on her neck, are not always what we would want them to be. Modern literature, you know, is not an idle pastime.

– You know, if you play your cards right, you could be killed on the premises, he said. I'd make sure you had a Quality Funeral.

– In Sydney? I do not want a funeral in Berlin.

– Perhaps I would just dump your elongated body in the botanical garden, he said, his fingers around her wonderful long white neck.

– Gardens require manure, she said. This body is just something to throw away, useless.

She turned it, and he said no, it is a long way from that, and he put his soap-covered hands on her hanging breasts.

5 · Going Under

· 61 ·

The local is eternal, even in a city that had to be built from scratch.

But men and women are unable to understand it. Most men and women. The human being is just meat that will not be as useful as a wheelbarrow of dung, while all around him, all outside him, is the local, the intelligent. All he has to do is leave his senses open and it will pass through him, enclose him. It would be like drowning in knowledge.

So he thought the day he was visiting the wall. At the Brandenburg Gate he hovered near an American and his son and their German guide, probably a business connection. The American man and his son were Jewish, from some city in the United States. How interesting this must be for them, he thought.

The American man put a polite question to his German.

−So, was this gate used as a checkpoint between the two Berlins before the war?

The German managed, just, to keep himself from shouting with his surprise.

−No, before the war Berlin was not divided into East and West. It was all one city.

− Oh, said the American.

His son did not say anything. He was wearing Adidas basketball shoes. He probably thought that Adidas was the plural of an American name.

The Canadian man was not surprised. He had heard an American visitor ask in Vancouver where he could get seeds for a totem-pole tree.

Well, he thought, as he looked left and right to where the wall went its way, grass and a barbed wire fence on one side, scrap dirt and discarded food wrappers on the other. The human nature alone is not all that smart. The thing is – oh, did I really say in my head, 'the thing is'? That I know this, something from outside lets me know this, but knowing this, how can I pick up the special knowledge this international organization of fiction-loving women, and who knows, maybe men too, was the sailor involved, certainly the Silesian drunk, if he was drunk, was, seems to share but seems not to want to divulge entirely or quickly enough to me, their, what, literary agent.

Good term, given the circumstances and the muddle.

He looked along the dreary grey of the Unter den Linden, grey because of the weather that was even cloudier and darker to the east, wondering where his trip would take him, trip him, probably to a dreary Stalinist apartment unit, one of the tiers of human filing cabinets he had seen from the reprocessed Pan-Am air above the city. He would be looking perhaps for a woman he thought he had nearly loved.

Now it was snowing again.

· 62 ·

What really bothered him was not any foreboding of danger.

Apparently he was being groomed as some sort of spy, if you can believe it. That is, where was his ordinary life, the commodity hours, where they and all that? Not exactly nine to five but some hour to some other hour, and the same path from and to his Kitsilano apartment.

What really bothered him was that while he was apparently (to him, he hoped, only) being turned into a spy, really, nothing was happening. He didnt even look around West Berlin all that much any more. A lot of that had to do with the central or eastern European weather. Who wanted to stroll Bismarkstrasse in the snow hurrying down out of really black clouds at a forty-five degree angle?

In spy novels, well, he had not read many of those, but in spy movies, there was always something happening, or if not happening, about to happen, and in the movies the music made it seem as if something was happening. Slowly things were being learned, and then quickly.

There was an intelligent operative, lots of experience to make him canny in his raincoat at some dock, probably, always at night. He was getting into the middle of whatever it was. He was a core of rationality or logic stepping into a world of chaos or the unknown anyway, stepping into the wild logos and sorting it out, bringing order.

That's how it is in a spy movie. A puzzle. But Annalise was right about puzzles and mysteries.

In real life, and his mind began the usual quibble about that term, in real life the mind of a man is not rational at all, not at all rational, no. The universe around him is logical and rational, and the reason it is unknown is because he is too savage to know it. A fool.

He remembered making love in and out of the pool at the hotel in Perth, and how he had felt that the English or whatever she was at last was his sanity. She was what encompassed him, opened up for a few hours.

It was crazy, but that was how it was.

Nothing happened this day. If Annalise did not return tonight nothing would happen tonight. He was alone and therefore thinking with his limited capability.

The green mottled telephone rang, and he stood up, took his only ashtray and a package of West, full flavour cigarettes with him, and lifted the receiver, the shape in his hand thick and perhaps soft, a nice telephone, though blunt.

– Hello, he said, or rather, hello?

A female voice coming from some distance, off a spinning satellite, said Harry? As if she were saying Hairy.

– Yes, he said, hello, who is this?

It might have been a voice out of the past, but he could not place it. It might have been a voice out of the future. So many of them were.

– This is somebody who cares what happens to you, Hairy.

– Doesnt everyone?

– No, they dont, Hairy. Especially that German one.

– Oh, great, he said. I dont know who I'm talking to, and already I have a jealous woman in my ear.

He put the thick receiver between his hunched shoulder and his ear and lit a West. Maybe next week he would be smoking an East.

– Hairy, the voice said, all this stuff that you think is happening, it's not really happening.

It sounded American. New Yorkian. Maybe Jewish Queens or at least Long Island New Yorkesque.

– Well, Mairy, here I am in Berlin, he said, like Bogart with a fresh cigarette between his lips. Do you mean all these cities and countries or all these women?

– All of it, Hairy. It's not happening. You are imagining it all.

– I'm safe in my Kitsilano bed, is that it?

– Oh, something's happening, Hairy, but not what you imagine. You just believe the wrong things.

– What are the right things, he asked. I'll admit that these things are a little scary when they are not tiresome. But I never had so many women wanted to guide me through the world.

She sounded awfully patient.

– There is more in the world than you know, Hairy. If you dont believe in it you dont know about it.

– You mean like God?

– Try gods, Hairy. Or something like that, she said. Remember what your mother said, poor thing.

She had been dead for ten years.

There was no one on the telephone.

· 64 ·

He was really testy on the streets on May Day.

Peculiar, on DDR television they spent hours showing a million people parading through Downtown, *Mitte,* smiling, waving at their old president in the horn-rimmed glasses and 1947 hat, all of them holding flowers or flags, the flowers must have come from Bulgarian hothouses, or eastern-Europe shaped paper cut-out doves, the wide streets jammed with happy German folk, atavistic but soviet, an odd and indubitable Germany. Hans Brinker better go into hiding.

But here he was on the confluence of streets around the Kaiser Wilhelm memorial church, failing at his attempt to get a bus pass for May, not many people on the blustery rain-threatened sidewalks. The sun had been shining bright on DDR television. Here it seemed as if there were few people on the sidewalks but every one was in his way, old widows in dark woven coats shaped like potatoes bound on crossing diagonally in his path, eyes staring at 1943, friendless and without power, but determined nonetheless. They never look at you, these people, and all these old people. But they want your space, you might be an inferior race.

He decided to go into the American chain hamburger

89

joint for some fast food. The lineups hardly moved at all, and he stood in his lineup for fifteen minutes, feeling pressured by the teenagers who edged around him, were they really going to push in front? Finally he threatened one, a light-brown-haired boy, and the boy said something in teenage German but did not recoil in fear, only edged a little slower.

Germans! He wanted to shout, Fucking Germans! and start smashing faces with his furled Roman umbrella. Get out of my space. I need some god damned living room.

Not just the Germans. Their ugly and stupid language, butt of so many jokes – I mean who would say pfoomff for the beautiful number five? And the clouds, dark, too low, always pushing down, the air refusing spring, refusing May, pushing in, cold and damp. The U.S. helicopters beating it against your ears and vibrating your apartment.

Now he knew what apart means, and he felt it but he could not get it, all this pressing.

But if a Yankee looked down out of his brown machine he would see just all one thing, Harry unknown and just unremarked, a part of it.

· 65 ·

One thing he kept doing in Berlin was turning off the light and going to sleep.

Wondering whether he would wake up in East Berlin in the morning. Wondering whether he would wake at all. Like a child, wondering whether he was asleep all this time, in a private world of impetuous phantoms.

When you are at home in your own seaside apartment, you tend to turn off the television and the coffee machine, drop your shirt and socks and shorts on the chair and fall into sleep, your body easily finding its usual posture, say lying on its right side, right hand under the pillow under your right ear, left hand in front of your face, knees drawn up a little. In three and half minutes you are asleep.

But when you are in a foreign land, in a temporary room you are getting a little used to, you ritualize it all, perform bedtime. Brush your teeth with the toothpaste you bought in Sydney. Hang your shirt in the wardrobe closet. Hang your pants with your other pants. Put your shoes parallel to the ones with the other colour. Throw your shorts and socks into the plastic grocery bag. Most clothes start with s. Set the radio alarm for, let us say, eight. Set the wind-up travel clock for eight-fifteen. Put on your pajamas. Turn off the overhead light. Get into bed, lying on your right side, imitating as much as you can your posture back home. Will they find you like that?

Turn off the light over the bed.

Outside it is three degrees. There is a light rain in the wind, reaching, once in a while, the unshuttered window. As if a sprinkler had surged.

Three and a half minutes.

When a man goes to bed he turns off the light himself. When he dies the light is turned off.

He cleaves to the darkness. He and the light are cleft apart.

He is fast, fast asleep. So slow, he is not moving at all.

· 66 ·

Every day he waited for the sun, and every day the northern winds blew rain in his face.

He was waiting for the sun because he did not want to go through Checkpoint Charlie or is it Checkpoint Charley, he did not want to go to the other side in the rain. He was Deutschmarking time in Wet Berlin.

And he hoped the sun would arrive on a day when there was a 'window.' He did not know quite what that meant, but his disinformants had said enough to hint that it had something to do with the schedules of certain people on 'the other side.'

He would like to be in the Andes, on the sunny side of the mountain.

Meanwhile he watched the couples negotiating the puddles on the German streets. One half of each couple was a short woman in a potato-coat. She was about sixty-five years old. The other half of the couple was a young man in his twenties. He was not visible because his body was somewhere else, sometimes in little pieces, sometimes just lying awkwardly in a broken mess of wet metal. They did not talk to one another much, but they were always together. They did not go out to dances or parties. Mainly they walked the streets.

The young men were much more attractive than the old women. They had got more attractive as the years went by, while the women became shorter and their coats got older. The young men had become so attractive that one might mistake them for Teutonic gods. They would live forever while their partners grew older and smaller and more fierce on the wet sidewalks.

Soaking Berlin was a city of souls that would never light up.

Yet this morning he had stopped on the street just outside the Oskar-Helene-Heim U-Bahn station to light a cigarette. Out of perversity he tried his lighter without hunching himself around it for protection of the spark. It caught right away and held a flame straight up. He was so startled that his thumb slipped off the little wheel. But when he tried it again it shone for him, beautiful.

–You in your small corner, he said, the words coming around his dry West cigarette.

Checkpoint Charlie was not difficult, only slow.

On the way there, on the U-Bahn, and walking Fried-richstrasse, he was excited, a little nervous, his heart racy, perhaps. Passing through, though, was not difficult, the shave-headed Americans in their temporary-looking booth were reading drugstore paperbacks. At the East German temporary-looking huts with their peeling paint and corrugated plastic roofing, there were no guns, not even any pistols on the belts of the uniformed border people. Everyone wanted to look at his passport, and there were no instructions about where to go next, but he just put on his practised genial and vulnerable look, and there he was in East Berlin.

None of it had been anything like a movie of 'international intrigue.'

On both sides of the border Berlin looks like a place no tourist would want to come back to. The buildings were jagged plinthes on the grey ground, and there were holes in the street, surrounded by chunks of old concrete and sheets of metal that looked as if they had been dropped there because no one wanted their large rusted ugliness.

In the drizzle he walked toward the showpiece Unter den Linden, and in a weak gauze of sunshine he walked east on that neonless boulevard.

It was Saturday afternoon. There was a window, apparently, but all the shop doors were locked. He wondered where he would be able to spend some of the twenty-five East German marks he had been obliged to buy, at par.

He walked and walked, until his feet began to get sore as they had during his first days in each city he had visited in the past few months. One went to cities hoping to be surprised by things one did not expect. East Berlin was filled with flags, the German flags with the compasses in the middle, and plain red flags. Each window he passed displayed posters proclaiming forty years of gratefulness to the Soviet soldiers who had made Berlin the 'Stadt aus Frieden.' There was more space than there were buildings. It was not Hell, not his, anyway. He was not dead yet.

When you cross the checkpoint to death, you will encounter such things as you had not been able to imagine. Here he was somehow used to the Mitte of Berlin, DDR, quite quickly.

But his feet in his blue Canadian shoes were bringing anew an old message. He was a middle-aged man and he had to sit down. He found a cafeteria where people were eating meat and potatoes at the Hotel Unter den Linden.

· 68 ·

You got your tray, and your meat and potatoes and beer, you paid for it with just a little of their flimsy money, and then you looked for a place to sit.

This was Saturday afternoon, and there were not many things for Berliners and other people to do here in the middle on Saturday afternoons. So finding a place to set down himself and his tray was not easy. He walked around the cafeteria once, past the windowside seats where people loitered with their obvious western cigarettes, then came back to the place where he had begun. There was a brutal looking man sitting alone with three unused places, and some empty beer glasses.

He grunted a question. The brutal looking man swallowed a reply along with some gravied fat. He had a great number of dishes on his tray, and his elbow in the air. Well, it is his country. Time to sit down, gently moving the beer glasses only as far as necessary toward the other's space.

He looked down at his goulasch and rostkartoffeln, and inexplicably there flashed before his mind the figure of the woman in the casket in Sydney. The silk around her neck. It was a shade of white he would not see here in this very different city. He applied himself to his appetite, fighting against the impulse to throw up when a piece of meat turned out to be fat, the kind of yellow fat that comes from some animal that has never fed on grain.

The brutal man was paying no attention to him. Now there was room to look at him. He was something between forty and sixty years old, wearing a cheap black leather jacket and a shirt with the kind of feckless design we associate with Slovaks.

The goulasch did not have enough paprika in it, but the potatoes, a kind of moist home-fries with onion flavour, were delicious on a Saturday afternoon, and they helped to take away the DDR money that had to be used up on this afternoon of closed shops. Wisely the Eastern Bloc countries forbid the bringing in of their own money. Not even Gypsy mothers would keep it in their hands in the west.

The brutal looking man slid sideways and stood on thick legs, then carried his devastated tray to the galley cart. As he did so, with surprising silence and speed, he caused a little square of brown paper to ride up onto Harry's tray. The latter was going to leave it on the corner of his tray when he put it away, but luckily his curiosity led him to pick it up and turn it over.

It was his first written message in a couple of weeks.

It said, in English, but in the German usages of handwriting that can be so baffling or at least delaying of understanding, window gebroken. Neue window buy at Flee markt, Sonneday.

· 69 ·

He always liked the idea of going to a flea market or a rummage sale, but when he was there he always hated the push and crush of the crowd, the impossibility of stooping to look at a red-stone ring without getting banged around sideways by the bent waist.

95

So it was here. He felt better in the slow lineup at the bratwurst stand.

The flea market was large and famous, beside June 21 Street not far from the the zoo. The stands, secured by guy wires made of thick string, were jammed one against the next, and there were five long rows of them, with jaw-to-shoulder crowds in the aisles between.

Once in a while he saw a young man carrying a house plant, long bouncing branches of leaves softly reprimanding Turkish moustaches down the long passageway. Once you got in there was no getting out, until you arrived at the end of the black-brown aisle, and then a flash of opal might well tempt you to turn and edge your way into the next hole.

He had thought that he might find a piece of lapis lazuli, maybe a lapis ring, and three times he waited and waited behind a widow in a potato coat, only to find out when he could lower his head and remove his glasses that it was only a black opal or a blue stone dotted with another colour. Well, maybe one of those *arbeiter* caps he saw socialist intellectuals affecting. But the only one he saw looked to be not good enough and not large enough. And it had no price suggested in writing. He hated that.

Still, here he was, in a press of hundreds of Germans and some others, wandering among discarded remnants of time, old portrait photos of farmers in uniform, grey magazines celebrating the machines of the early twentieth century, worn and chipped leather greatcoats that never were any good.

He had come around the world to be here. What if someone made the natural mistake and tried to buy him? He was here, after all, and free to be just about anywhere else in the world. He was meant to be here, an item of refuse, fake bargain, maybe he was born to be here. Character is fate.

Well, he would not dive into that mob again, no matter how enticing the Peruvian beads hung higher than even German heads. But here was a book stall, right at the end. Waiting this time for the slow scan of the prematurely grey young man in the brown overcoat that should have been unloaded here today, he thought at least he could buy a book to read while he waited in the glamour city for something conspiratorial to happen, and who knew when Annalise would reappear, or anyone? Today it looked as if at last and for once one of their corny written messages had not worked. That seemed probable, after all, in the real world, and we will not get into the tired debate about that place. Blood on the dining room floor, indeed.

There was as much English literature as he had expected. He had read it many years before, but he could not remember much about it, save for the usually attributed clichés, that being *Light in August* – he certainly hoped so – by William Faulkner. It was the same edition he had bought for two dollars a quarter of a century before, the Modern Library edition, with a dust jacket only slightly chipped. He paid five Deutschmarks for it now.

And now that he had actually used the trip to the flea market, he could go home. Home?

· 70 ·

Home.

Well, it was getting that way. The stains around the sink were layered. He heated up the coffee in the saucepan and poured it into the cup with stains of two days ago in it. All the other cups were in the sink. Not true, only one was. Plain fact is that he was the only person living here, so a dirty cup didnt matter. There werent any flies around, yet. There was no blood on any of the floors yet.

He didnt even look to see whether the money was where

he normally hid it. Any burglar would know where a person hides money; just has to know whether it was hidden by a man or a woman.

Yes, this was a pretty low-key spy business, if he was a spy. He didnt even have a gun or a fake passport. All passports are fake. Forget it, that's as bad as the chestnut about real life, almost.

The higher the stakes, the higher the loss.

But he had no real life knowledge of the stakes. Some short stories? A female athlete with fake hormones, another kind of passport. Weird DNA in the DDR? And what did he have to lose, besides time and a pail of dignity?

If it were a pail of water he could put his hand into it, and then take it out and see how much of a hole he had made.

Well, time, then. He would sit down now that the coffee was probably cold, but still German, and read his book.

It was not *Light in August*.

It was perhaps a little heavy in May.

A late spring.

A little dark in May?

Inside the Faulkner dust jacket was a book just the right size for it, not a completely common thing.

It was not a printed book. It was a bound notebook, on whose pages were written, in several kinds of ink, some early, apparently, drafts of fiction. He recognized the fumbling sentences. They were the sloppy gene pool out of which the peculiar book of stories about female athletes had been fished.

You had to hand it to them. They must have done a little research on his phobias, his reading habits, and the locations of bookstalls.

Now he had the longest written message they had got to him yet. But he was not an interrogator, not a critic, and, he thought, not an espionoliterary scholar.

· 71 ·

Here it was, the fortieth anniversary of VE Day.

He remembered VE Day, he thought, remembering a
newspaper headline, but that would have been at least one
day after VE Day, because at age seven he had been living all
his life in Williams Lake, and at Williams Lake in those days
you were lucky to get the Vancouver papers the day after
they were published. When he had moved to the Coast one
of the strangest things was to read last night's hockey scores.

So what did he do on the fortieth anniversary of VE Day?
He sat on a bench in the Berlin Zoo, reading the Hague edition of the *International Herald Tribune*. It contained the
hockey scores of two nights ago.

The orang-utan huddled under a burlap blanket. She was
squatting in an old truck tire, and her lidded eyes beheld the
other side of his newspaper without discernible emotion.
She was, the sign informed one, born in 1947.

This was his first visit to Berlin. She, while he had been
travelling down to the Coast and then around the world, had
been in a central European world. She has been in it nearly all
her life. The burlap covered her head and nearly covered her
eyes, still gazing red woman. For here there were steel bars
and glass walls and no concept of Europe or Victory, or justice.

He read through the light entertainment columns on the
last page, no mention of Schklovski, and threw the thin
folded newspaper into a trash basket, following it with his
plastic coffee cup.

Now he had to return to thought, so he put his hands
behind his back and walked by the rest of the ape and mon-
key enclosures, not seeing them as symbolic at all. That is, not
until he noticed that the gibbons' space was surrounded by a
ditch and that the ditch was enclosed by a white wall made of

verticle slabs. It looked like the Berlin Wall, all right, except that it was not rounded at the top.

He had to return to thought, though, and of course he thought about the book of handwriting he had tried to read last night. It was difficult because the English words were written the way that Germans write them. He had trouble recognizing a K and an H, for instance. But he recognized the fumbling sentences.

He would try to read it again tonight, and try to ignore the developing part of him that was impatient to make the sentences more easily idiomatic in their English.

· 72 ·

He could not find a Thai restaurant in Berlin, but after looking at as many animals as he could stand at the zoo, he decided to go and eat one, and for this purpose began walking up what would be Kantstrasse, sure that everything he saw along the way actually existed as an independent objective fact.

He would never find a Thai restaurant there, but he found an Egyptian-Italian restaurant, believed it, and sat in it for an hour, eating something with labial fricatives in its name, and the first rice he had seen in the land of the potato salad.

No justice for the orang-utan in the tire. But still, he could not shake the idea that justice will catch up with all subterfuge. It was very naive for a man of his age, living in this postwar age. As a child and even as a young man, he had made a fetish of telling what he thought was the truth on all occasions. Even the smallest lie would be found out. Even a dot of rot can begin havoc in a sack of potatoes.

But fiction? What is a lie in fiction? If, let us say, a person pretends to be someone else, let us say she pretends to be a well-known writer of fiction, and let us say – he sat back in his chair as the Egyptian waiter arrived in the fashion of an

Italian waiter – that she publishes some stories under the name of the well-known writer. She may be living a lie, and telling some lies to so live it. But are the stories then lies, in themselves? If they are, what about the stories written by the English, let us say, writer of fiction herself? She was certainly not a reporter of independent objective facts, you cant deny that.

Maybe when he got home he should burn the book instead of trying to read it. Burn them all, maybe. Just burn. Fire is going to get everything sooner or later anyway. The end result wont be changed.

Home?

Till the end of his mild dinner anyway, he would pretend that he had made up his mind in favour of the fire.

· 73 ·

Keep your eyes open, keep your ears open, get ready to learn something, even if the balls of your feet are bruised, the small of your back aches as soon as you get up in the morning, and your cock is only now recuperating from the intercontinental bruising it has been taking this quarter.

– That's all your typical dream, the voice on the green telephone had said again at four in the morning.

Was it someone calling in the evening from North (or South!) America, or someone calling from the afternoon in Australia? He had amazed himself by cursing in German into the thick receiver.

Of course he had not burned the manuscript, if that is what it was about.

Even if he could not figure out what it was trying to tell him, if such an egocentric view could be sustained, he felt as sure as his sore eyes that there was something there. Something someone thought might be worth half a million Deutschmarks. Deathmarks. The Spot.

101

He then noticed that it was eight in the morning and he could smell German coffee.

– One, how the hell do you get in here, he shouted, his feet groping for his old leather slippers, and Two – oh shit, I forget two.

– Do you wish me to slice some of these strawberries onto your corn flakes, she asked.

– And oh yes, Two, he said, where the hell did you disappear to?

She appeared at the bedroom door, in a white mini-skirt and wrinkled white cotton shirt that bagged at her elbows. She looked wonderful, and that made him grumpy.

– I have been to London, she said, to visit the queen.

– I am afraid I know what you mean, he said.

– Do you always sleep with the shutters up, she asked, refusing the end-rime.

– It's broken, he said. The sun never wakes me, just relentless women and B and E practitioners.

– B und E? You mean bacon und eggs? I am afraid you dont have any. You will get cornflakes and strawberries. C und S.

– Shit, he said, pushing past her to get to the toilet.

– Then please close the door, she said, going back to the kitchen.

– How was England, he asked, as he joined her, wearing his pajama bottoms.

– The sun was shining, just as here, she said.

– It's about time, he said, taking a taste of the cornflakes; then he dug in, careful to lift one piece of strawberry with each spoonful.

– Oh, it shines all the time, she said. You may not be able to see it, but it always can see you. The sun never sets on the British or the Empire. B und E, she said.

– What are you on about?

—The fire in the sky. You can never escape from something that never sets.

—Yeah, especially if there happens to be a window, he said.

Now he was learning to talk like a spy, anyway.

· 74 ·

But fire cools and is converted into earth, into, finally, our clay bodies, our ashes, if you like.

—I dont like cigarette ashes in dirty dishes, she said. Why dont you get an ashtray or two for this place?

—I keep meaning to steal one from a café, he said. I like the ones with Teutonic inscriptions all over them. But I keep forgetting.

He got up and held his cigarette butt under the tap, then tossed it into his garbage, a plastic bag from Meyer's grocery store. He thought of India.

—Just divine, she said. Your life is so spiritual.

—Okay, Ms Spiritual, he said, lighting another West. Tell your humble savant what you were doing in London.

—I told you. I was visiting the queen.

—Did he welcome you?

—I told her I was a literary journalist. From Bremen.

—Was he suspicious?

—Well, she does have a new book of stories due to be published in the summer.

—What?

—It is a selected stories. Apparently there is one new story, and the rest are taken from her earlier books. The best of.

—The new story. Did you get a copy of it?

—No, but I do not think you will find the roots of it in your manuscript. She and her friends, if she has any, will have created it in England over the last year.

He was staring at the end of his cigarette, as if looking for

103

divine inspiration. He settled for a deep drag of smoke and air.

– You know, he said, I still cannot believe it. I wont believe it until I see her naked again. Him.

– Were you sober in Perth?

– More or less, he said. Though when we were together it was like –

– Indeed, she said.

– It was like truth at last, I thought.

– And the American sailor?

– That was neither truth nor falsehood. That was stupidity.

– Stupidity and a strange ocean, she said.

– I'd like to forget that.

– Ah, she said, everything that is, is holy. Didnt anyone ever tell you that?

He stubbed his cigarette butt into his stained saucer, as if to refute the possibility.

– Beautiful, she said.

· 75 ·

No, he was not a literary critic.

He was not even a literary man, though living in Kitsilano he had some acquaintances who were literary, or at least literate. At least he saw them carry hardback books with them into the laundromat.

Not a literary man, but from time to time he would read a real book. Quite often, if you consider the national average. If you make acquaintances, you sort them out, till the ones you maintain tend to concur on books, music, food and sports. For instance, to take a most immediate example: Conrad, salsa, snapper and boxing.

Really, though, not a literary man, at least not to the extent of pretending one could become even temporarily a literary critic or scholar.

Then why were these two lines, of poetry, presumably, going through his head, the way the first radio song you hear in the morning hangs around all day, and more than that, added to that, who ever wrote them, presuming that they did not come to begin to live all at once, spontaneously and independent?

> *Man is in love, and loves what vanishes.*
> *What more is there to say?*

Maybe, he thought, getting, ludicrously, entangled in global intrigue, that seems paltry except for the money involved, leads one to recall or invent such pronouncements, even to use such an ambitious noun as 'man'.

Poetry is someone's voice speaking to you, and if you are not a servile consumer of pronouncements, you will, when spoken to, speak back. Having got through all the commas. Even if a passerby would mistake your reply for prayer, there being no human figure standing in the direction toward which your voice goes. As if, that passerby not having all the present information, you were addressing gods or heroes rather than poets.

But he could only speak to them as if he were chatting with a wall, say the wall of a thirty-year-old gothic church, or the wall around a city.

A long time ago in Europe the people inside a city erected a wall around it to keep the others from getting in. Now in the century he thought those two or nearly two lines came out of, the others had built a wall around a city to keep themselves from going in. That is not what they said, but that is what they did.

What vanishes?
—I been psyched by the best of them, whatever they are, he boasted.

If he had seemed to be on the trail of death in Rome, the eternal city, here in squat phoenix Berlin there didnt seem to be any death.

No tombs of the great gone, no ruins older than forty years, no bunker, no fire pit. They were all alive who had ever lived here, and they were celebrating life. One did not see that in the faces of mothers with baby buggies in the subway, their faces staring out of not enough sleep. But there were their babies, American, German and Turk. Living like crazy, not that far from uranium.

He was as they say killing time in the museum of Indian Culture in Dahlem-Dorf. In front of him for the last little while had been an immaculately lettered rectangle that said, probably, *Teil einer Naga-Balustrade. Angkor Wat. 12 Jahrh. n. Chr.* It was on the simple pedestal below a chunk of mural showing a humanoid creature with its companionable arm around a risen and flared cobra. Humanoid and cobra were wearing satisfied mischievous grins. Enjoying life.

As a child he had been a self-instructed Christian, a kind of lonesome neo-Thomist Protestant. But he had never been animated in any negative way by pagan worship. He thought pagans were people buried in the Biblical past, in the Bible, as a matter of fact. The first time he heard an American voice decry pagans on the radio, he was astonished that some arcane people thought there were still some around. He figured that the term must be metaphorical or allegorical, this boy who would not grow up to be a literary man, like calling teenage gangsters vandals or huns. Later he heard a Catholic believer, from a European family moved to Williams Lake, refer to non-Catholics as heathens, and he rather suspected that the term would even designate himself.

Eventually he himself became a kind of Christian non-believer. Then when he saw middle-class youths in Vancouver dress up as some kind of pale Hindus, he could not credit them with actual devotion. No more could he believe in the beliefs of Catholics at Christmas, or rose-carrying dreamy-eyes in airports, or American Blacks decked out in Arab prayer fabrics.

What they called mysteries were only embarrassing noises and a nuisance to people living next door.

So what about those East Berliners in their ecstatic parade of life on May Day television? Did they believe, or as American radio preachers believe, are they cozying up to the wall, waiting for their main chance, but shrinking away from the band of unapologizing death?

· 77 ·

On the other hand, how was he different from them, the bourgeois esoteric?

We love what is always vanishing, is that right? The women he was meeting and sleeping with all over the continents, they could be depended on to vanish, that alone. But did that have anything to do with love. One of them, yes, she had something to do with sanity. Or so he had felt. Now he was almost certain, if he could follow the story, that she had once been a boy at least, possibly a man. An athlete, certainly, never a god, and then a woman? A writer of short stories?

Had the boy died then, when the woman was born, in that clinic in Leipzig?

Well, we are all dying. Do we know any better than the young on the Ku'damm that death is just a respectful name we'll eventually have to offer to the god even now known as night-life?

No, that boy had not died for fun. He had died because

107

there was a worm inside him, a worm that wanted wings on its segmented body, a woman, a world champion.

He was, as he often was when he could no longer stand the empty apartment with the yellow trains rumbling by, walking down the Ku'damm, West Berlin's magazine article street, where the sidewalk tables were at last out in the sun. When he could not face another dutiful tourist project he went to the Ku'damm and walked past all the stores with linen jackets in the windows, their sleeves rolled up, hung on stylized mannequins. Where wide older women in perfect jackets walked manicured doggies attached to their hands with expensive leashes.

Every time he had made, what is it, love these past few months, he had been thinking somewhere in his head that they, the women, were helping him celebrate the climax of his life, the last season.

He felt like Marlowe's pooch.

Walking down the Kurferstendam, he noticed after a while that he had been following a tall slim woman with light brown hair that rippled to her shoulders as the thin heels of her pumps struck the thirty-five-year-old sidewalk. Unusual hair for Berlin, where most of the young women had it shaved up the sides and back, or dyed orange and exploding sideways from their pates.

If he had been a literary man he would have felt quite descriptive.

He followed her until she sat down in a yellow plastic chair. He walked on by. Then, making a gesture of delayed decision and maybe some resignation, he turned, came back, and sat nimbly in a yellow plastic chair.

· 78 ·

Her apartment was in an old building that had escaped the bombing and the fire after the bombing.

The wooden floors creaked when you walked on them. The morning sun came through cracks in the old grimy shutters, and left stripes of light across her endless narrow back.

There were specks of dried blood on the twisted sheets – not from her, but from the scratches she had made on him, when she had almost made him quit but forced him to go on, to proceed, he thought he remembered her saying, forced him partly with her filthy language, her brutal threats and vulgar requests.

He thought of kissing her gently from the top to the bottom of her long spine. That seemed a gentle thing to do after the hard night, though.

If anyone had seen them he would have thought them mad, not knowing what they were doing, would have thought they had lost their minds to some goddess of night disease.

Turning back and sitting down on the yellow plastic chair had led to this, marks and pain and a desire for more, sometime. In a bloody world he would cure himself with blood. Threatened by flames on the near horizon, he would set a match to himself. Covered with the excrement of the dying, he would drop for comfort and purification into the sewer.

She was not the sewer. She was soon awake.

– Good morning you fucking prick, she said.

– Are you going to say good morning to the rest of me?

Then she did, and the pain was excruciating, but he dare not tell her so, tell her to stop. She stopped when she forced an ambiguous climax from him.

Later, safely clothed and sitting with her at a tiny wooden table on her balcony four floors over the loud street, he asked her whether she had a message for him.

– You got the message last night, she said.

– That's all?

– You want more, Liebling?

– No. No, I mean you are not part of the editorial board?

She did not deign to reply to such a stupid or obscure question. Then why, he asked her, did she take him home?

She opened her mauve-painted lips over teeth that themselves looked a little coloured. Her hair rippled in the morning slant of light.

– I want to enjoy myself while I am young, she said. I have lived all my life in Berlin.

He felt that it was a remark made to people who were intended to receive instruction in such modernisms.

– You mean this was an entirely gratuitous incident?

She put down her white cup and with all ten of her long slender and powerful fingers seized his hair and forced his face down toward her endless thighs.

· 79 ·

So maybe the editorial board had not sent a message through that beautiful vulgar woman of one-and-three-quarters metres in height, still not enough to look over the wall without help, but enough to see an hour into the future and go there.

Have fun while you're young, a duty.

But maybe it was a message after all. Stalin works in mysterious ways his wonders to unfold. Hitler's Third Reich still had nine hundred and fifty years to go. The Sibyl is obviously demented, her eyes wild, her mouth and tongue slobbering, her words dark and coarse and ugly, but she speaks a truth that will overcome human prejudice and human hearts in a thousand years because a god or goddess is always speaking through her.

Oh he was tired of religion, rough as it was. There is still a swampy Teuton devil in this ground, even while the enormous doves perch in the low branches of the Tiergarten. He

110

was tired of mystery, of puzzle, of disappearing women, of wads of currency, inferior fiction, tired of his own story, he was tired of strange dark wet vaginas.

Who would have believed that? Keats lay in his hole, a skeletal virgin. Verily, martyred women who once smelled of cheesy maidenheads lay honoured in the cold soil under warm Rome.

God, or a god, or a goddess, or his own unacknowledged soul, his shadowed wisdom, had a message for him.

– Pan Am, it said.

– Lufthansa, it whispered.

6 · Going to Ground

· 80 ·

Mistaken as they may be about the singularity of their thoughts, all people do think.

He thought that he would like the information he had to be more clear. When he got around to reading books, let us say novels, he preferred sentences that were clear and straight and not too long. Faced with a choice between a self-regarding arty novel and a book that kept its reader, who bought it, informed of what was happening all the way through, he preferred the latter.

If all people think, and thinking people recognize that other people are also thinking, it should be obvious that they would be serving each other and themselves well to say things to one another with clarity, to reveal everything they know about a given subject of discussion, and to cover the subject in order, from alpha to, say, omega. From one to a hundred, or a hundred and twenty-four, if that is how long it takes.

If one of these women were there right now, that is, in the downstairs cafeteria of the Dahlem Museums, he would make that argument. Even better if they were all there, the silent woman in the Thai restaurant included. Restaurants.

But it was his experience that women do not argue, that they do not like to argue. They are all hunger and no appetite. Women do not like to argue. They like to fight. Some men, he supposed, like to fight too, but he did not think that he shared a mind with them. They seemed foreign to him, part of the surround, and not too close, either.

But none of those women had tried to fight with him. They were more given to enigmatic remarks, like professionals who saw no likelihood of your being interested enough in their profession to become an adept. Like the photo-engraver who smiles at you and says 'magic' as he produces his wonderful artefact.

I like to explore my faculties at large, said Mata Hari. There is a new sun every day, said Tokyo Rose. Get home, said the English short story writer, who was not any of those things, and perhaps didnt qualify anyway. Even with her history of qualifying.

Why didnt just one of them say we want to use you to get someone home if she wants to get home?

· 81 ·

He found a Thai restaurant in the phone book, by looking up 'Thai' and 'Bangkok,' and even found the name of its street on the back of his map.

Look, it said, at 4B. He scanned the square under 4 and across from B. He looked at it right side up and upside down. He rotated the map ninety degrees, over and over, around and, that is, around, and ran his fingertip over all the space. He could not find the street with its long German name at all.

North east south and west. What's the food that we love best?

First he was frantic. Then he was angry. Then he was frustrated. Then he was disappointed, partly because he had not had Thai food for three months, and partly because he thought he just might learn something in a Thai restaurant.

114

Might start all over again, or erase the past three months and a bit more, right back to the beginning. It seemed to have been a beginning.

This time he would run as soon as he saw her, drop his chopsticks on top of his meat salad and bolt through the kitchen, out the garbage door. No, he would accomplish the same avoidance more neatly by not going at all.

He would drop his chopsticks onto his meat salad (he hoped it would be good and hot) and run straight at her, grab her with both hands, all the time trying to disguise the action not as a scene but as a lyrical episode, for all the other diners, imagining that this Thai Restaurant, Ahornstrasse 32, would not be empty like the one in Sydney, and he would sit her down, or better, take her outside, to the nearest greenery, and make her tell him in plain sequential common language what started all this, and what was his part in it, and why him.

– First there was fire, she would say.

– No, he would say. No koans, no riddles, no self-referential narratives, no puzzles, no mysteries, especially, and no evasive fucking.

– Consciousness is how it is composed, she would say, trying anything to avoid explanation.

– No, he would say, we must all speak clearly and logically, and thus share rational discourse, as in a short story by Graham Greene or some other English writer. We must have a body of thought and speech in common, just as the people of a city live under the same laws.

– You are wrong, Yank, she would say.

– Dont start that, he would say. The laws of the city derive from the laws of the orderly universe, which are more powerful than any of our skulking and disappearing. And the same thing goes for language. So tell me in plain English what this is all about.

– No spickee das Englische, she would say.

But if it is a law descended from the orderly universe, why does it need defending?

Defend the law and love it, as you defend and love the city wall. That magic circle, is it still unbroken? Are we still one within it? Does the god or goddess rest easy on our faith?

They used to build a circle around their city, magic to keep rapining foreigners outside. But here for the first time the foreigners have built a circle around our city to keep themselves out, and here inside we have dug tunnels to run back and forth in yellow trains.

Near the wall Hitler's Third Reich rests under the topsoil, a city of tunnels the foreigners could not explode, a bunker in which no one goes anywhere, unless the foreigners have now tunnelled a connection. History goes back and forth.

But do track stars and short story writers? Across all sorts of magical curved lines?

He was pursuing these feckless thoughts while riding home on the Krumme Lanke-bound No. 2. Across from him a teenaged blonde girl leaned her ripening body against the little wall that separated the long seat from the doorway. She looked as if, eyes half-closed and blonde hair scattered in front of her forehead, she would burst with the desire for the end of a long sexual ache. He saw a letter C inside a circle stamped in ink on her hand and not yet washed off or worn away. She had been at a pop-music concert or a dance the night before, and had not let Saturday night get as far as it wanted to. Now on Sunday she was avoiding eyes as people do on elevators or the U-Bahn, but looking through lowered lids at his legs and more particularly.

She looked as if she could have been a healthy young athlete but was doing something else instead, and not enough.

They had managed to drop a magical circle around him, and it was well closed, like a law.

Well, he could still burst out. There was no real bond holding him. Except his curiosity. And that night in the swimming pool in Perth.

· 83 ·

He was thinking of the little man with the big horn-rim glasses in the funeral parlour a few steps up from Oxford Street in Sydney.

He had said we were expecting you probably yesterday. When he said we, had he meant we the funeral parlour, or we the people who are trying to get an English writer out of East Germany? Or could he have meant we the people who killed the woman with the Formosan silk around her neck?

It was probably she, he had decided then, so what of his fantasy now? There would be no more of that woman in Thai restaurants. But if she had died in Australia, and if she had been killed, then the peril he was facing or had his back to now, was not across the wall on Leipziger Strasse only, not a matter of his choice only. He could get into trouble on a lone night in some U-Bahn station over here.

He always stood well back from the edge of the platform in any city. Now he would try to keep his back against something, a wall or a pillar, something stationary.

He had only once seen a policeman in the subway, and he was just going home from work.

So the law did not extend underground? No, the police, despite their rhetoric, are not the law. The law is the principle that gives people a single will. But here in Berlin that had been tried and tested with dreadful results. So now the power in uniforms tried to stay invisible or casual. In front of the enormous U.S. consulate there was a single German police guard, a man who stood half in the shadow, trying to

117

appear as if he had just stopped there to have a look at the traffic or the moon.

Gut Tag, he had said the first time he had seen this individual. A stingily offered grunt was all that came back. On the other hand, when he had given a pleasantry to the heavily armed and helmetted U.S. soldier in front of the officers' club, he had got no response at all, just regulation arrogant U.S. silence and observation.

In East Berlin the uniformed men walked around the Alexanderplatz, carrying packages.

He was sitting in his apartment, looking at his damp clothes suspended from coat-hangers hooked to the central light fixture and a ledge of the radiator.

The telephone rang loudly.

He got up and lifted the chubby green receiver, and said hello in English.

There was no answer.

He said hello twice more.

· 84 ·

Coming down the stairs and onto the ravine platform at the Dahlem-Dorf U-Bahnhof, he saw a robust man standing beside the control booth.

A plastic sack of groceries hung from one of the man's hands, and nothing from the other, which did not exist. Only an empty sleeve left to hang rather than being pinned up or tucked away. He was healthy-looking, and seemed to be about old enough to have been a teenaged defender of the city in March of 1945.

It would have been nice to look to left and right as he approached the man, as was his practice, to seem to find the mauve lilacs on the bank of the ravine of interest, or the advertisement for the Dallas Symphony Orchestra pasted to the cylindrical imitation kiosk. Unfortunately, he had slept wrong on fresh linen last night, and all day he had had a sore stiff neck. When he turned to look at something he had to turn at least the top half of his body.

– Oh, poor man, said the burly stranger with very little accent but lots of sarcasm in his voice, oh poor *man*, you've got a stiff *neck!*

He wanted to look around. As far as he could see the platform was deserted save for the two of them. Otherwise he would not have been worried about what to look at. Otherwise the man would not have spoken to him, at least not in this manner. But someone with soft shoes could have followed him down the stairs. He felt embarrassed about the fact that he was holding the handle of a white plastic sack of groceries in either hand.

– Oh, I feel so *sorry* for you, said the man, doubling over with feigned grief.

– *No comprendo*, he replied, wondering where he had got that idea. *No lo entiendo. Yo no hablo* German.

Shit, what was it? Alemánia?

– Oh, God! – The man was louder, and now there *were* people coming down the stairs – To wake up in the morning less than *perfect! Que lástima!*

He looked to see whether a yellow train were coming. This really hurt his neck. One was coming, in the wrong direction. He might take it.

– In my opinion one man is worth ten thousand men if he is only as complete as *possi*ble, if only he is the best there *is.* Do you not agree?

– *No me moleste!*

This was a grumbled whisper.

Someone opened the door of the train going the wrong way. He got in fast and sat down, the bags on the floor beside his feet.

The burly man was at the window, saying something he could not follow, the empty sleeve pushed up against the glass.

· 85 ·

The next day he scouted the wall.

First he got onto the No. 2 S-Bahn, which cuts through the western projection of East Berlin and then runs along the western side of the wall to Frohnau, the Gartenstadt, northern tip of the French sector.

He had decided the hell with it, he would go for the excitement, the enclosed glory, the silent fame, rather than another decade or two of quiet productivity and reward. These were going to be his most remunerative years. But if you are going to have a midlife crisis this late, you might as well act it out. Time to quit being a Canadian.

Taxi drivers dont have most remunerative years, anyway.

The No. 2 S-Bahn becomes an underground train as soon as it enters the East. It has to dip to get under the wall, and as soon as it is there, it stays in the dark till it comes out again into the rubble-strewn free world. Also, it picks up speed, hurtling, as they say, in the uneven dark, past all the deserted subway stations with their dimmed lights, stairways sealed with cinder-block walls, and lone DDR guards.

The train goes at a terrifying rate so that no East German citizen who manages to find his way down to the spectral platform can grab hold of a passing car and be hauled safely into the sunlight.

Okay. Now he knew that.

Only the Friedrichstrasse station is now operating, but it is a customs stop, well populated with guards and featuring long lineups of westerners at the Intershops, people eager to get rid of their flimsy DDR marks and to go home with inexpensive trinkets and alcohol.

Then the train whips by dark Oranienburger Str. and Nordbahnhof, and back into the light. Soon they were travelling along the wall, built next to a lower and older wall and separated from another wall by two hundred metres of bare earth with tank-traps and gun towers above and anti-personnel mines below. The new apartments on the other side had white curtains in the windows and lots of television antennae on the roofs.

This was not the place for glory. He wondered what would happen on the other side if he came here and threw the half-million beautiful western Deutschmarks into the air and over the wall.

He saw a back-hoe reaching over the high wall and picking up a bar of concrete from the old wall. There were three uniformed guards standing very close and watching. Usually they worked in pairs, presumably not good friends. They must look into one another's eyes a lot. Presumably they needed three here because there was a chance that one of them knew the back-hoe operator. Or maybe because this civilian was a lot closer to the rubbish-strewn west than people usually get.

The village centre of Frohnau is the end of the line. Here he got out and walked eastward, the strap of his Italian leather tote bag across his chest, and today's *Herald Tribune* rolled in his left hand. It didnt matter – it could have been in his right hand.

He walked past expensive new houses with nice landscaped gardens, Audis and Porsches parked in front of them. Tall trees, willows, pines, were in every yard and along the narrow parks between the boulevarded streets. It was as if, so close to the East German ex-urban wasteland, capitalist success had a duty to exhibit itself, even if no one from the country lanes on the other side could see through the concrete.

He got to the wall by taking the little driveway that was the end of a street made of wealth that began to disgust him but then left him indifferent. He saw a sign that declared in French and German that this was the end of the French sector and that furthermore there was some danger.

There was an informal path of beaten earth that led into the willows. He ducked between and under some branches, and there he saw the wall up close. He could have touched it, but he did not. It had no graffiti on it out here in the suburb. And it was low, less than three metres high.

From the other side came the noise of a defective engine, a motorcycle or one of the sad automobiles he had seen and heard around the Marx-Engel-Platz. He thought about throwing the illegal *Herald Tribune* over. The only other reading material he was carrying was a book of essays by Mordecai Richler in his bag.

Instead he took a piss against the wall. He was probably the nine hundredth person to do so today.

When he turned around to go back he saw the old concrete posts. They were in two lines running among the little trees. They had once had barbed wire strung between them, two metres high.

He was technically in the first few metres of communist territory that ran uninterruptedly eastward until it came into sight of Alaska.

He could have been famous.

· 86 ·

Just this side of the wall, fenced off and a little obscured, there is a monument to the Russian soldiers that brought their gawky bodies into Berlin forty years ago and met bullets from the last of the German children with ammunition.

On the other side of the wall is a graveyard with an enormous monument, the kind communist planners like,

122

something utterly without taste but with such size that the sophisticated can only mumble their disdain, fearing the brute strength of the organization that put it there.

Those that die in war used to be held in greatest honour by men and gods. Now they are shamelessly commemorated by civil servants and bad sculptors. Bad in the sense that they have never imagined anything better; or bad in the sense that they ignore their imagination and allow the satraps to win the war between bureaucracy and art in a walkover, never even leaving any mines in the fields of retreat.

He was looking at the first-named monument through a fence, as close as he could get. On the fence there was a sign proclaiming this bit of fenced forest to be part of the British sector. The piece of roadside property was Soviet, though. On it was a gigantic golden Russian soldier and two little green armoured tanks. These were two of the first west-bound vehicles to pass through the Brandenburg Gate on that day in May forty years ago.

There were also three people inside the enclosure. Two Soviet soldiers standing like bits of sculpture, and one German workman with a bucket. He was applying a new coat of green paint to one of the tanks. Honouring those fallen in battle.

What will they do for me if I dont make it back, he wondered. What will my own people do if I dont get the half-million through the customs check?

My own people?

· 87 ·

He had always thought that in the spy business there were rivals, men, and who knows, also women, who were jealous of their reputations, who put everything on the line for their reputations.

– You heard about that business in Tashkent?

– Yes, of course. Was it – ?

– Scherbe.

–Of course. That bastard. Should have died ten times already. Scherbe. The – ?

– The Tashkent Syndrome.

But the truth had to be that most operations – embarrassing word, once he had thought it – were what, carried out, that's it, by people such as him, people with no reputations at all. An apartment dweller in Kitsilano, a printer's son from Salem, Ontario.

Maybe he would develop a reputation in the next few days.

He hoped not.

· 88 ·

He was riding the S-Bahn to Friedrichstrasse because he thought that there he would not be a lone walking figure as he had been stepping over the desolate ground at Checkpoint Charlie.

Did the Easterners call it Checkpoint Charlie? Unofficially?

Why was he doing this? Lots of questions today. Where have they gone, the snows of 1945? Why *was* he? People who look into motivation, novelists, psychologists, police interrogators, have a list, and they check through it, Charlie.

The European-old train car with its curved blond wood inside was just about full of travellers, some obvious Yankee couples in their clean styleless clothes. Some workers, the huddled masses of Europe one hears about in one's childhood. Europe, Europe. When he was a child that peculiar word full of vowels meant war and intrigue and odd-looking machines. Some young women in torn leather pants and shaved heads, the usual amateur tattoos. They would be passing through to the suburbs of the Free World, where they probably had rooms in their parents' houses, and pet dogs with clean hair. He always wondered whether there were any Easterners on the way home, professors and art critics with permission slips from Moscow. Or maybe you know who. He had not been keeping a look-out, and now he wondered whether two of them, say, had been keeping him in sight for weeks, and whether he, an amateur he now knew for sure, despite the games he had once played, would have had a chance to notice them. Had they been watching his lonely walk up and down Leipzigerstrasse then?

Money? He didnt know whether he would come out of this with any money, though he had all along supposed he might. He was distracted or bashful, and he never asked. He did have two hundred and fifty thousand Deutschmarks, twenty-five soft old bills stashed inside his underpants. He hoped the border officials were not of a bored erotic state of mind.

He wondered whether to state that he was carrying a quarter of a million marks. If he did they would nab him because of what he was likely to do with all that lusted-for hard currency. If he did not, and they decided to look at his nude form, they would nab him for certain. Lots of questions tonight, then.

Love? For whom? For a woman he had read but never met, though on another continent in two other hemispheres he had thought her uncomplicated ardour had put an end to his experience of probably madness.

The train plunged into darkness surrounded by munitions. His heart was pounding as if he were a child. He could, couldnt he, stay on the train and ride to the West again by going north, rich as he had never been, at least until he returned south and then went west, to the airport at Tegel, leaving his clothes and camera in his apartment, where the telephone would ring at six o'clock, and would they bother, because they would have thought of the airport. What about the airport at Schoenefeld, a flight on a loud, large Russian jet to Baghdad? Never been there. Fuck love.

Patriotism? He didnt even know what nationality all the editorial board members sported. One of the English short story writers was East German, and one was English, or had been when last heard of.

Pride? Now that was just barely possible. It had certainly led to his doing unrecommended things in the past. But this one thing he knew: you should step on pride and put it out faster than you would put out a fire.

Insanity?

· 89 ·

I did not come two-thirds of the way around the world I still have some affection for to turn away when knowledge might make itself available, he said to his body that was pressing itself against the curved wooden seat.

He urged it and coerced it and then flung it surprised out of the car and onto the platform. Surrounded by dirty concrete, a bunker beneath the tidy streets of the new order.

It's only human beings, after all. Only like human beings who have made what you are entering. They cook your sausages, in a manner of speaking. They print your theatre program. They build walls and hide tanks behind them. They are all afraid, and the only thing you should be afraid of is the thing more resourceful than human beings.

The woman in the ill-fitting green and yellow uniform did not ask him whether he had a quarter of a million hard Deutschmarks tucked around his fundament. Only whether he had any books or magazines.

– Only this Baedecker, he said.

126

And he was up on the street, in front of a grand looking hotel.

But of course he wondered whether she had been instructed to let him pass easily.

However, now on the street he was exhilarated. No, he could not be simply walking the steps they wanted him to, assented to, the western they or the eastern they. He saw the wide pits made by bullets in a massive Baroque wall, and stepped close to take a photograph of them, so close that his color picture would be only grey. That gave him a frisson. Would the watcher be insulted?

Yes, now for this hour at least, he was glad that he had decided to do it, and no longer needed any speculation about motivation.

Because if he were home if that is what it still was in Kitsilano, he would be doing whatever he had done some previous week at the similar time. Similar is worse than same. He would be controlled all right, not by some editorial board or some acronymic security agency, but by the very routines that squeezed the time of his life together into an amalgam of boredom.

Oh, he might hanker for that routine from time to time. But those times were similar. This one was not. Is not. It is not even time at all. If the conspirators check their watches it is not to hear the time told. It is to see who is still alive, to see whether the death of earth has resulted in the life of fire.

· 90 ·

Hark hark the dogs do bark, the beggars are coming to town.

Some in rags and some in bags, and some with a fortune wrapped around their cocks. He would stay away from lonely sailors today, here in the vast flatlands of north central Europe.

127

Lots of German shepherds in Germany, but no sheep. Invisible shepherds patrolling the death strip at the frontier. Just like the ones around the edges of the soccer pitch.

Everything becomes sparks. Everything becomes marks. Ask at any *sparkasse*. A fair exchange admits no larks. No birds, no jokes over the wall.

Yes, dogs will raise their unpleasant voices at the appearance of a stranger. He had been nothing but a stranger for months.

In West Berlin dogs were citizens. At the airport returning parents say hello to their children and shower kisses on their whimpering jumping dogs. In the parks the hairy dogs outnumber the naked young people and even the old Turkish women, heads covered by dull cotton scarves.

But here in East Berlin the only dogs are shepherds pacing among the landmines, looking for invisible sheep, barking in athletic support of the bullets that keep people at home where they can support the burgeoning economy.

I am an innocent North American tourist, his body posture said as he strolled to the Alexanderplatz and dutifully looked up with appreciation at the new hotels and shopping emporia. He kept the practised look on his face, too, the melange of naivete, vulnerability and ignorance. He consulted his legal Baedecker, his head bobbing up and down from page to gold-lettered church across the way.

My my, no peasants' hands, very good. No decrepit tractors and rifle-toting Russian bull-dykes. Very modern. Very tolerant of religious history. No giant portraits of Lenin on the hotel wall. Look how bare the girls' legs are.

I dont know, maybe I just *will* go and visit the monument to the fallen Soviet soldiers. Maybe these communist people did help bring down the Nazi scourge after all.

In the highschool drama club he had been one of the school's premier thespians. But in the university players' club he had been among the worst actors to strut the boards. In more recent times he had been a little more successful in impersonating a taxi driver.

· 91 ·

They must have some individual brains left, but do they?

What remains of common sense, what fingers to reach from their intellects? To follow the words of their singers as if they were thought, to enter huge crowds parading behind the band and smiling radiantly up at the stage, as if the crowd, so many crania filled with cells, were wisdom, as if the crowd were a teacher. They forget that when there are many they are bound for error, and the good are few. And those few are not thrown up by the crowd, are not up on the stage.

So he thought, wondering a little whether he were right. Here he was in the west of the east now rather than in the east of the west. Berlin and Trieste and that other west. That's what brings you to sharpened perceptions and muddled thought.

Here he was in the *stadt* of conventional behaviour, looking for an odd individual. Bizarre.

But it was best to ambulate for a while, be a tourist once again, innocent and tired, abroad and bipedal.

He turned into a doorway, found himself in a single room, and saw no one else but a young man in Trotsky glasses, a silent curator guard. This was a little museum or rather display called Lenin in Berlin. He walked around, from beginning to end, dutifully looking at everything. Displays of important modern history can be boring, and this was boring. So he didnt try to read the hand-written letters, just stood in front of them long enough. The photographs. The few personal effects. He leaned forward when he thought it advisable, tucking his camera into the small of his back so

129

that it wouldnt knock against the wooden display counter with its glass top.

The young man couldnt give a *scheiss*. He retreated to a little alcove with a mud-coloured curtain.

Drab. The common adjective offered by the neon west to describe socialist Europe, and it came up so far that he whispered it through his teeth.

Well, that's something, he thought, and making the tiniest of smiles for the expressionless youth (sullen because he hated this job, or hostile because he believed in it in the face of wealthy busy unimpressed westerner) and went back to the humid street under cloudbank.

· 92 ·

The local is eternal, but men and women are unable to understand it.

Most men and women. In a strange city you see things you would not notice if you lived here, details of the street most citizens ignore.

You are like a tape recorder that picks up all the ambient sounds as well as the conversation, so that when you play back the tape you are astounded by the noise you hadnt noticed when you were speaking, the background that is now up front.

But when you are in a strange city you see things you do not understand, and you look for things without knowing when you will see them. Well, of course it is simple, you simply – , says the local man you have stopped, but the directions have piled uncertainty on uncertainty.

And when your briefs are full of currency –

Once Homer, the noticer of things, was told by some boys: what we can get our hands on we throw away and leave, and what we cannot get our hands on we take away with us. He was utterly at a loss to know what they were talking about, but it was simple. They were looking into each other's hair for lice.

Harry got onto the proper S-Bahn at last, and headed for Treptower Park, a significant resting place of greenery, where one could view both the enormous monument to the Russian soldiers of 1945, and the western frontier of the Democratic Republic, known on its other side as the infamous wall.

The dead are not arrayed in neat rows with their particulars neat above them. They are packed into five grass-covered geometrical mass graves, the same fate the war's lovers would have designed for them. But some of them, on a rise, were buried in a vertical posture, standing at attention. Their vigilance still needed.

At exactly sixteen hundred hours he heard the ridiculous code-words.

– There is a new sun every day.

And at sixteen hundred and twelve he was among the trees, with a man's hand in his underwear.

· 93 ·

– When do I come to Leipzigerstrasse, he whispered.

He was whispering it to the man who had shared his table the last time he had been in East Berlin.

There were no visible guards anywhere, no Russians, no Germans. The only other people there were some ill-dressed tourists, either faithful rustic Poles or Bulgarians, clustered in front of one of the gold-on-marble quotations from Joseph Stalin.

– Get home, said the man, counting the bills, then reaching for the last few thousand.

– Home? Well, forget the ironies. Home? I was told Leipzigerstrasse, he said. Number fifty-nine.

131

A bird trilled as if it were safely in West Berlin.

– Things happen more faster than you think, said the man, licking his finger before making a final count.

Methodical greed was more animating than dark socialist eros.

– I really wish I knew what was happening, he said. What will I say to my, well, superior?

– Get home, the short blocky central European repeated. You will attend for the name of a city.

Then he walked away, down the straight path between the straight lines of straight trees.

So he was left with a cruelly tidy memorial and a cluster of intouring Slavs. A gigantic Soviet soldier made of dark grey metal or stone stood above them, carrying a naked child in one huge hand, the other allowing an outsized double-edged sword to rest on a broken swastika that resembled an angular snake in mortal trouble.

A thick hairy hand inside his gaunchies was not his notion of the perilous glamour of European espionage.

Deighton should be hauled out of the best-seller lists and flogged, he thought, and Le Carré with him.

On the walk back to the S-Bahn, feeling light around the crotch, he stopped at an *Imbiss* stand in the park. There was a souvenir stand as well, and he had twenty-two worthless marks to get rid of. But there were no souvenirs worth keeping. One might as well throw away the aluminum coins as throw away the shoddy goods they could buy here. He would find the same thing true of the Centrum department store. The whole of East Berlin with its aluminum cutlery and bulky jogging suits was like an enormous K-Mart.

He ate a fatty weiner and drank a bad beer with a smudged label.

Well, you have your good days and you have your bad days.

That's what the baseball manager says when someone sticks a microphone in his face.

Yesterday on television he had watched the news after the baseball game on the black and white television set he had purchased, as they say, for fifty marks at the U.S. Army goodwill store around the corner on the street with the name so long he would never remember it, buying with it a transformer for sixty-three marks so he could receive the right number of volts or whatever the electric charge was, and there was the aftermath, as they say, of a tornado that had twisted right through a town in Pennsylvania, a bad day in an ancient tornado path that could have brought a bad wind any day of the twister season. Someone with a microphone had obviously asked what it was 'like.' The man standing in a pile of angular boards and black and white objects was angry but also an American with a television camera pointing toward him. That is, he had to, like a baseball manager, entertain his fellow citizens.

– It was like a tornado, he said.

And you could detect anger at the question, and gratitude for the attention.

Behind him the town looked like a K-Mart turned upside down. People were looking for their valuables, but there werent any.

Now he was riding 'home' as he did every day on the No. 2 subway toward Krumme Lanke. As he did every day, though this day he was riding home from the Deutsche Demokratische Republik, the film used up in his camera, lots of room for his ass in his pants. He was wondering whether it had been a good day or a bad day. He had delivered the Deutschmarks but had come back empty-(well), handed.

Sitting across from him was a very tall young American, blond, mustached, in shorts and an old baseball shirt with the word 'Bears' on one side of the chest. He was sprawled over the banquette, his long bare legs spread across the aisle. Big meaty Yankee male youth. He was asleep, his head on a hand, elbow on a backpack that was beside him. Hard not to look at.

But when they stopped at the Dahlem-Dorf station he looked past the sleeping blond hulk's shoulder, that Aryan dream nightmare, and looked at the grassy bank leading down to the tracks. There, tucked against a weed, was a baseball.

He looked again, or rather harder. He leaned a little forward, not wanting to lean too close to that Yank, and yes, it was a baseball.

Good days and bad days, the manager said, having won or lost, he could not remember which. But he had been wrong anyway. All days are alike. Filled with details, all specific, all meaningful, some to you, some to me, some to neither.

· 95 ·

You will attend for the name of a city.

He had just about had it with cities and their names. He was just about ready to let the English short story writer spend the rest of her days in whatever city she was now a prisoner in. There, he had finished the sentence he was thinking with a preposition, one thing you're not supposed to admit to.

Somebody was going to a lot of what seemed like overly Byzantine trouble to get her back. He wondered who, how high, as they say, did this operation go? Did anyone go to London to visit the Queen?

One thing he knew was that if it were a Canadian short story writer who had been switched for an East German

134

sprinter, it would be hard to organize an editorial board. Even for a novelist who had been switched for a Marathon runner. The Canadians might as well get themselves to a shopping mall and let the country be governed by children. They are ready and willing to ban their best artists and thinkers to Los Angeles or Washington or London, because they cannot bear to have a star at home in the north. If you think that you are better than anyone else, they say, you can just go and live somewhere else.

Then why was he, a Canadian in a manner of speaking, working as a talent scout for this international editorial board? It was not even a countrywoman who had been Shanghaied.

Things happen more faster than you think.

Then why was it that he spent most of his time waiting for the green telephone to ring or waiting on the street for someone to whisper something to him?

Yesterday he had stood on the most crowded corner of the street, next to the stairs leading down to the Kurfurstendamm U-Bahnhof. The wind was blowing skirts against fat bellies. The ice cream stand was doing a multi-coloured business all the same. A woman appeared out of the crowd and into his eyes. She was not dressed flashy, yet not like a K-Mart Easterner, just ordinary small town clothes on her ordinary body. Her eyes looked anxious.

She's crazy, he thought. No, not crazy. Lonely. No, lonesome.

But when he looked at himself in the jewelry shop window, he had already composed his face, eyes and all. He looked like a Boston lawyer on vacation.

· 96 ·

He had attended, and the name of the city was Amsterdam.

This came over the green telephone, in a voice he knew.

135

– Why cant you go yourself, he asked.

He had never wanted to go to Holland. The only night he had ever slept in Holland was due to an accident of the weather. Seven or eight years ago he had sat in the Milan airport for a day and half a night, waiting for an hemispheric blizzard to finish. By the time he had got to Amsterdam ...

– That's for me to know, said the voice.

... his CPAir jumbo had long ago left for Vancouver, so he'd spent the night with two stranded Irishmen, drinking theretofore-unheard-of drinks in the bar of a hotel next to the airport. He had not slept for two days, and that night he slept for only two hours, and now he was glad not to remember the flight over the pole.

– Very original, he said. All right, but this will be the last flight I'll take for you people.

– Thank you, Harry. You're a dear. But you might want to take one for yourself, a little later. We will pay for it, of course.

– Oh God, thank you, he said.

But she was gone.

As usual there was a ticket in his name waiting for him, this time at the Dan Air desk at Tegel. As he was sitting over his shoulder bag in the departure lounge he saw a ticket agent and two German policemen surrounding an obvious Yankee.

– I'm not in your jurisdiction, said the obvious Yankee. I know my rights. You cant do this to me. I'm an American citizen!

Oh no, he thought. That had to be a line.

After he got inside the BAC1-11 and buckled his belt he saw the obvious Yankee get on the plane and sit down, somewhere behind him.

Oh no, he thought. They are finished with me, and now they want to tie up the loose ends.

Was it going to be on the plane, or in Amsterdam? Or was

136

the obvious Yankee a diversion, so he wouldnt notice someone else getting on the plane?

Unfortunately, he didnt think of that until he was sitting
high up in the front of the gingerbread in his room at the
obscure Washington Hotel.

He had always imagined Holland as a European Ontario.
All the Dutch people he had known could have come from
milk and cheese farms around Tillsonburg. Where they
would have told any of their sons who showed signs of
artistic ambition: you want to be Rembrandt? Go to New
Amsterdam, leave Canada to us nice quiet people.

Damn Canadians, he thought, knowing that Holland was
full of them, vacationers gloating over the Liberation of the
Lowlands forty years ago. Damn Canadians, I hope you get
good and rich, cheeseheads. That's the worst condemnation I
can think of for you.

· 97 ·

Amsterdam was by no means, anyway, a European
Ontario.

It was simply what people at parties had told him it was,
the city one would go back to on the next trip to the continent. Figure that sentence out later, he told himself, and later
he changed it to what it is now.

Amsterdam in the bright warm sunshine was cute, yes,
and quaint. Along the street-sides went girls on heavy old
bicycles, carrying violins in cases on their backs. Unlike them
and their obvious perambulatory purpose, he got turned
around and lost over and over in the jumbled diamond store
streets, and there, below the funny gingerbread housepeaks
he found the cuteness saved from eventual revulsion by the
hipness.

Tired as he was of cities, he already allowed that Amsterdam was one of his favourites. He had been told to wander
and sight-see, and at two in the afternoon to go to the

137

Rijksmuseum and look at paintings until three, presumably while someone looked at him to make sure there was not a third party or more looking back, or looking at that particular looking. He did not find this really exciting, so one is not alone.

Amsterdam, with its little blocks put together so neatly because since 1250 A.D. there had been no room for loose fittings, was a perfect place for a puzzle. But he was too tired of puzzles to try to put another together. If it wanted to be solved with him in the middle, all right. He would like some mystery, perhaps, instead.

But these Dutch masters were not much on mystery. Even Vermeer's window light on a woman's cheek was a matter of solving, a problem. The little cracks in the old oil made the painting look like a completed jigsaw puzzle.

Vermeer's light. Rembrandt's shadow. Each makes the other. Looking at the paintings – was this chiaroscuro? – he didnt know it, but he thought of what these past few months had eventually taught him, though he had known it, he now knew, since birth. We see the darkness all around our faces, sometimes invading the planes of our faces, yet we think we see a reason for putting our faces into the available light.

In the bright sunshine of Amsterdam you can see the black shadows under the bridges.

Life is doom, and we know it. Each day we step closer to our graves. Yet we light another cigarette and put our faces into the light, cherishing that life. And then, knowing that we are giving them the gift of death, we bring children out of the mystery into the world, into this puzzle, send them on their way to doom.

7 · Pass Go

There she was, wasnt she?

There she was, as he had not, except in the taxi in Perth, seen her, sitting down. She was sitting on one of the black couches, where she could have a long look at Rembrandt's Jewish wife and her possessive husband, at least the parts of the large painting visible off and on while the trance-walking tourists stopped for a moment, being as polite as their once-in-a-lifetime visits would allow them. But she was not looking at the painting or even the tourists. Her hair, with twists of grey falling here and there around her large head, so unmistakenly English, he remembered with tenderness, didnt he?

His heart was pounding. He could not get a message to his feet.

She might have been looking at something, so still was her face, none of it in shadow. But one could see that whatever she was looking at was not in the room, a room made, after all, to hold things people had wanted all their lives to see. A stranger would assume that she was exhausted by her holiday trudge, that her quiet stare was the usual traveller's hiatus.

Months before, he had known that she was his sanity. But she had been the first to tell him to get home. Now his body, inside itself, in any case, was shaking crazily, and he was

ready to insist that he cast himself away forever from everything he knew, only to follow her wherever she might be
living.

She was entirely still. He felt as if he would shake himself
to little pieces, till cracks appeared all through him, as on
Vermeer's dried oil, till he fell into a heap of fragments, like
one of those old cartoon cats unsuccessfully pursuing the
cruel clever mice.

In the hotel in Perth they had come together from opposite directions, each nearly half way round the globe, and
when they were in the pool together they had become water,
they had remained fire in their element. They had played the
most harmonious music possible in each other. What they
had played was not knowledge, but wisdom.

Then they had gone to the airport together, and from
there she had flown to Africa, and he had flown to America.

Now he had to figure out how to get across five metres of
Dutch floor.

· 99 ·

He now knew how much he had missed her, how
unhappy was his separation from her, now that she was
within reach.

Unless crossing that clean floor would prove to be more
difficult than crossing all those oceans and continents. So we
recognize the dearness of health when we are sick. So a slice
of toast with a dab of margarine is so wonderful when we
have gone without food for two days. So we cherish a familiar chair when we are exhausted from walking or running
through the streets.

So he loved her.

And she did not move. She sat still, looking at the thing
that was not there, until he stood with the toes of his blue

140

shoes nearly touching her brown shoes. Then she rose to her feet. He took her into his arms as she fell toward him, and as her unfamiliar scent entered his nostrils he saw a man standing by the glass exit door, looking at him with contempt or a nasty boredom on his face. Then he saw the man no more. He saw the glass door.

There were more white strands in the brown hair than there had been. There was no disturbing energy passing between their bodies.

– Who are you, he said.

Her voice made its soft way up the fabric across his chest.

– I am –

Not she.

– You are the real one, arent you, he said.

Surrounded by paintings and lights and people heavy on their feet, looking at the paintings, the Yankee teenagers walking in diagonals, unequalled boredom and ignorance on their faces. Their parents' chins working regularly on their chewing gum.

– I understand, she said, that you are to authenticate that. Then take me to the airport.

– Are you...?

– I have no luggage, she said.

· 100 ·

The man who disappeared from the Rijksmuseum doorway – was he the same one he had seen picking the paper money out of the Trevi Fountain?

Or just a quick-disappearing type? Do they all wear those sideburns lower than their hairlines? Is the Pope a Vaticano?

Well, people like the Pope are always talking about justice for all the people of the world. But who ever thinks of justice except he, or she, who is experiencing what seems to be injustice?

Whatever brings an end to injustice, it is not justice. It is,

141

usually, money. When you go without food for two days, it is money that buys you a sandwich. It is money that brings your relief from injustice, and finally you settle for an end to injustice, and you are not really interested in justice, only the end of injustice.

On the yellow train to Schipohl airport he tried a few times to engage her in some talk, perhaps a little enlightenment, and he was confused about love. It would have been nice to find out what got her, and him, into all this.

This he knew: an East German athlete who had been the best in the amateur world at his sport had had a sex change during his trips to the west. Then when his hormones had ensured that he was no longer the best man at his event, he had tried to persuade his government to let him represent them in the women's event. Well, said his government. I need another year of treatments, he or she had said. No, said the government. Then I will tell the story, he or she had said.

Are you a good story-writer, they had asked.

No, that is not what they had asked. But no, they said. We have another solution that entails your disappearance. That was, of course, given the recent history of his country, unsettling. But then they had added: and entails your reappearance as the teller of stories you seem to desire to be.

So much for plot.

But how did they get you to East Berlin, and why didnt they simply arrange for *your* disappearance? That is what he wanted to know from her. So he tried to make small talk, leading up to it.

– How long have you been away from England, he asked on the train.

She did not say anything for a long time as the very green fields went by.

Then.

– Wherever I am is England, she said.

A great many details, please.

Sorry, too late, she is already home in London, and there is the BAC1-11, a stumpy DC9, waiting at the end of the little portable tunnel, and here he is with half a plane-load of silent Germans, ready to brave the corridor, the corrida, once again and take the U-Bahn home. No one is rich. No one is poor. We are only ordinary people doing what we have to do. Fish in the sea. In our necessary element.

No, he decided. There are elements and there are elements. The ocean for instance: fish can drink it all day long, but it will kill a poor Canadian who tries to swallow more than a human share.

International espionage, for instance: there are those who thrive on it, who make a more than comfortable living on smuggled paper and disappearing princes. Then there are the rest of us, who perish in the first exchange of documents or gunfire. Or soon after that, anyway.

Now the British-made jet was climbing into the dark clouds over green Holland.

– This is going to be my last eastward flight, he said out loud, but not too loud.

I will gather my dirty socks and Pentax and get back across the frozen waste to the edge of the blue Pacific.

But when he got onto the No. 9 bus at Tegel Airport, a woman came and sat beside him, though he had hoped that his clutch of bags and suitsack would deter such an event.

– I was going to wait for you at your apartment, she said,

143

perhaps a little lewdly, but I couldnt wait that long, so I decided to come to the *flughaven.*

– But you didnt go so far as to carry my bags to the bus, he said, not smiling.

He did, though, experience a little bit of an erection, of all things, for which he thought he felt also some impatience.

– I admit that I wanted to observe you a little, without being seen myself. You know, you look a little tired. But you were successful, I have heard.

– Oh yes, he said, scrabbling to get the falling straps of his bags over his shoulders as the bus slowed for the Jacob-Kaiser-Platz U-Bahnhof. But I dont know what the hell I was doing. And that poor English woman if that is what she was seemed to be lost to the world of serious literature. All your efforts and plotting may have been in vain, as far as British letters are concerned.

– Ah, but you neednt worry about that, she cooed. You did your part well. You acted successfully.

– Like a fish out of water, he said.

· 102 ·

By the time they had got to his apartment, he was feeling wrung out, as if he would fall into a pattern on the floor, like chestnut blossoms after a heavy rainfall.

She did not help him carry his bags, but she placed the palm of her hand against the small of his back as he climbed the two flights of stairs.

It was a little humiliating to feel drawn so hungrily toward a person who manipulated his life, sent him to cliff-edges and rifle-ranges, and left him ignorant of the reason why. He watched her take her white cotton jacket off her shoulders, and saw one tanned German breast through the scooped arm-hole of her light yellow blouse. A yellow blouse against deep-tanned blonde skin would have been enough to set his heart racing.

He thought he knew what was good for him, what he valued most in the world. That was to leave her behind him forever, to get home as fast as he could. In the meantime to stop his ears against any of her blandishments in that damned beautiful German accent.

But his body remembered the lift of her little belly, the shine on her wet teeth when she opened her lips to smile as she grasped him. If she touched his tired body he would immediately forget the attractions of westward air travel. A donkey would choose soft hay over a purse of gold.

He resolutely carried his bags into the bedroom, and started unpacking, throwing his used underwear and socks into their plastic sack with the word Meyer on the side, hanging up his shirts and linen jacket, putting his radio and shaving kit on the little table.

That is when he noticed the apartment. Everything was neat and clean, the bed laundered and made up, the parquet floors gleaming, very German. He went from room to room, looking at dusted lamps and fresh dishtowels, and a vase full of new flowers, tiger lilies.

Then she came out of the kitchen with a picnic – sliced ham, sliced cheese, sliced white bread, a bottle of *Deidesheimer Herrgottsacker*. She put it all down on the coffee table, pushed him down on the couch, and bent her head before him as she removed his shoes from his sore feet. She rubbed his toes and his soles and his insteps.

– Will you marry me, he asked.

She laughed lightly, then shook her bushy hair away from her face.

– Of course not, she said. The life you live is much too dangerous for my taste.

It was the next morning, of all things.

The goosedown quilt was lying across them sideways, and the big pillows were on the floor. His left arm was completely without feeling because her sleeping head was on his biceps. After a night of jumping and bouncing and sliding and twisting and then sleeping, her hair looked as it did in the middle of the day, a tawny bush spreading away from both sides of her face. She was snoring lightly. Her mouth was open just a little, and there was a gleam. She looked, as the cliché has it, and despite her occupation, innocent as a creature just sent from God via the forest.

He liked her a great deal. He wished that he loved her.

She was lying on her back as he was, with her strong but small hand high on his thigh. He picked up her narrow wrist and lay her hand palm down on his reproductive organs. And now she was not asleep.

Afterwards they talked. He told her that he liked her a great deal despite everything. She averred that she felt similarly about him.

– It is too bad that this is all over, he said. I'm going to miss you.

She licked at the moisture in the hair at the middle of his chest.

– It is not over, *Liebling*. Our avaricious agent from Leipzigerstrasse is waiting for the second quarter of a million of hard marks.

– You have left a few of those on –

– Too obvious, Harry, darling.

– You are right. Why not just forget the quarter million? He's already rich beyond his worker's paradise dreams.

– You see, I think, he has great expenses. In an affair such as this, he has many people to pay, and some of them are still waiting to be paid *their* second installment.

– Let them all go, he said, his hand admiring the gleaming contour of her forearm.

– No, Canuck. We must maintain our reputation. You see.

– You have more fiction writers to redeem?

– No, but we have to keep an open account. Anyway, I dont want to oppress you with all the details of our association. You will require a clear head for your visit to the Pergamon Museum.

– I'm going back over there?

– If you would, please.

– Oh yes. Iron Curtain espionage is my element. To me, voyaging through the dark corridors of the Warsaw Pact is my daily bath.

– I knew you would grow to like it, she said, looking flirtatiously at him around the edge of her hair.

– You, he said. Chickens bathe in dust. Pigs bathe in mud. I perform my daily ablutions in the death of earth.

She moved so that no part of her skin was touching any of his.

– I wish you to be additionally prudent this time, Harry.

– Oh yeah?

– Yes, this time you must meet him at the Pergamon Museum, and then *you* choose the place for the exchange. So that he is not in danger from them, and so that you are not in danger from them and him.

– Oh, this makes me so happy, he said.

– Yes?

– As happy as a cat in water, he said.

· 104 ·

Now it was raining every day.

There are fewer things, he decided, more dispiriting than waiting for a window in the rain. He went to the zoo because the subway went right there, but a zoo is nasty in the rain. The animals that care huddle indoors, and it is dark.

She was still six feet tall and Annalise was still an interesting name, and she was simpatico, but for some reason he avoided her a little, even when she was at the apartment.

He looked at the poor female orang-utan again, the creature sitting in her truck tire with an old sack over her head. Definitely an animal person, but ugly to the human gaze, to the erotic imagination. The most beautiful ape is uglier than the ugliest human being. That's what they say, and it is true.

Once again, last night, he had heard the female voice on the telephone. Harry, she had said, as if she were saying Hairy.

– Yes, Mairy, he had said.

– You are still not seeing what is really happening, Hairy, she said.

– Do you still advise looking to the gods to see what is really happening?

He was tired, but here it was, a voice, anyway.

– That was your way of putting it, the voice said, sounding like the voice of someone's unloved aunt in the Bronx.

– I have learned quite a lot more about what is happening, he said.

– You're imagining it all, the voice said.

And then it was gone, replaced by the sky over the Atlantic Ocean.

Whom the gods will inform about what's happening they will first drive mad, he thought.

But why should *they* care? The most beautiful human being still looks like a Barbary Ape next to the plainest of the gods.

That night he buried his lonesome penis in her bushy hair. He gathered her hair in both hands and moved her head down. She smiled, but he only wanted to wrap his lonely penis in her wonderful bushy, tawny hair.

Most people, she had once said, dont really know what is happening to them, or around them, but they think they do.

You, she had said, are not really a fool, just your usual, a man.

She was not his real love, but he did love being with her, annoying as it could be. If he was imagining all this, he liked the progression of his imagination, at least from the Pearl of the East to this Prussian taskmistress.

But his real heart was in the pool in Western Australia. He was admitting that now.

Annalise, though. No one quite of her sort anywhere. He was perhaps a toy for her. A little boy being told what to do. A child in this grown game.

And what about the gods, so-called? Men, and even women, are only children in the hands and plans and sky-scapes of the gods. Remember, he had told himself many weeks ago, the Berlin Wall was after all built by mere men. From the air it looked like the wall of dominoes children like to make.

What about that hairy-necked man over there waiting for the second two hundred and fifty thousand Deutschmarks? Was he aware of how much like children's solemn games this all was? Or does an unseen machine gun aimed at your shoulder blades keep you in an adult world where death is not the running out of quickness but rather mere human conceit?

He remembered the young boy who had guided him home from the beer parlour in the east end of Vancouver. Maybe it would be interesting to ask her the boy's name.

Then for a moment he thought: are women gods? No, no. But women do not build walls. Have you ever heard of a woman building a wall? They might find a wall and espalier a pear tree against it. Or contrive to have purple blossoms seem to spill down its face.

What a lot of reflecting he was doing. How little is happening. Waiting for an expensive window. Propping open the doors of perception.

He stopped at an *Imbiss* and bought a nice tight bratwurst with a lovely line of mustard down its length, and thought of the other boy over there, eating a fat-filled bockwurst.

And the gods, the women, smiling a little, indulgently, or looking in another direction entirely.

· 106 ·

Something kept bringing him back to look at the wall and over it.

He had been twice to the other side, and would go once again, maybe forever. It was just ugly concrete, seen from either side.

If there is justice it is created by war. All right. If there is beauty it is there after a history of war. Agreed, with reservations.

He looked at the lapis lazuli ring he had finally bought yesterday. Lapis comes from Afghanistan and Chile, two countries ruled by killer tyrants, at the centre of mass state violence in our time. All the poets, they say, love lapis lazuli.

He was standing with a few strangers, a Yankee old enough to have been in World War II, and some young Brits, on the platform raised for tourists who want to look at an open stretch of the death strip just east of the wall. Dont come in, it said. He had been here nearly two months ago. Since then some brave but imperfect grass had come up in the flat space between the high walls.

Birds, some magpies, some other crow-like creatures, soared over the wall. There were two men in an Eastern-

Europe-looking jeep driving slowly along the hard tracks laid out in the death strip. Sometimes they stopped and got out and disappeared together into holes. Then there was other movement in the peculiar enclosed landscape. A young rabbit scurried across the grass and stopped still, disappearing until one's eyes settled on the spot. Then another rabbit appeared, and soon, getting used to looking for them, one noticed rabbits all over the open space between the walls. They didnt know where they were. They were presumably too light to trip an anti-personnel mine.

Such observations are bound to set off a rumination of a philosophical sort. One might go like this: under the eye of God, a.k.a. the logos, everything is good or at least beautiful; but human beings are doomed to divide things, calling some beautiful and others ugly, calling some good and some bad. Generally the bad is supposed to belong over there.

Below the chimney pots.

He was to go over there tomorrow, in broad if not bright daylight, to the museum of antique politics, to throw good money after bad. A man vaguely in love, frightened and dulled in the source of his trouble.

What about the notorious growth rate of rabbits? Did they eventually become the quarry of hunters and eaters, and if so, at what hour of the day or night did the shooting occur?

· 107 ·

He woke up the next morning and had a conversation with himself because there was no one with him this day.

It was probably planned that way.

– I am not looking forward to this day.
– Oh no? You would rather be home, driving your hopeless cab through the nice weather, past all the populace on bicycles?

– Rather than trying to save my life in the probable rain in this flat city.

– Flat as a pie, cut in half. Are you hungry?

– No, I just wish it wasnt today. I'm not looking forward to this day.

– Then why do you have a Hugh G. Rection?

– That's normal. Means I have to take a leak, that's all.

– But what about symbolically? Up for whatever presents itself, all that?

– All that presents itself is our godawful obsession with that wall.

– Fuck the wall.

– More of your symbolism?

– I dont know that much about symbolism. But I'll concede on the wall. It might be the reason for all the bad weather.

– You know, I have been thinking like a bourgeois taxpayer about the wall. Those citizens over there? They had to and have to pay for that thing. It's very large, and must be expensive to maintain, I mean purely in terms of Eastern marks, and what do they calibrate? Man-hours of work.

– Person-hours. Citizen-hours. Patriot-hours.

– Yes. Do you think I should get up and have a leak now?

– If you can manage to get it aimed at the bowl. Is that all you were thinking about the citizen and the wall? No symbolic figure?

– I am not a literary person. I am a cab-driver and an international agent. Both against my will.

– Well, you could have said this, for instance. The authority that erects, excuse me, the wall, is like a doctor. He cuts you and burns you and poisons you, and then he has the pluck to present you with his bill for his questionable services.

– That's old-fashioned. That sounds like a doctor from the ancient world, or the medieval world.

– The world when cities had walls around them.

– How –

– Clever. Thank you.

– That's not the word I was reaching for.

· 108 ·

Looking at three-thousand-year-old writing on Assyrian steles or tablets, black stone in the Pergamon Museum, he wondered what story *they* had to tell.

The writing looked sharp in the hard dark grey, rather, stone, looked as if it just could not be thirty-one centuries old; it looked that way especially in contrast to all the print he had seen over here, the relentlessly drab magazines in the one magazine store he had found, the ticket for the museum he had put into his pocket and which he knew had already become a ball of lint, nearly.

But not for long, he did not wonder about that story for long. There was nicely printed currency, two hundred and fifty thousand Deutschmarks in his blue underwear, useless detail, and here was the swart man again, pretending a citizen's interest in a fragmentary Assyrian shield, and there was a broad museum guard perhaps pretending disinterest, stepping back and forth from foot to foot, pretending too that he was not bored. He had to be one or the other, something.

The swart man would not be able to do him in here, not in such a state treasure. But what about, yes, the Bulgarians with their poison umbrella tips? The swart man was not carrying an umbrella, it was a cloudy day, but it didnt look like rain, not when he had come in, and this was not Britain, where one carried an umbrella anyway, and the swart man was not a Bulgarian, but even though there was uninventive bureauocracy they did not likely use umbrellas anyway, anymore.

And what about what he had thought of on the S-Bahn to Friedrichstrasse? She had said that he should be careful on this trip because now this was the last of the money for this transaction. But she had said that they had to send the second installment for their reputation, so that some future deals would not be endangered. As the train rumbled eastward he had not been able to focus his brain enough to decide whether that were a contradiction. Or a contradiction to be frightened by.

Who, what, who was she, in the configurations of some they or theys? Was he a rabbit?

And he was here now. He had to lead the man somewhere where he could give up his rich groin and at the same time or rather as soon as possible manage to get back across.

The East Berlin rule declared that the visitor must return by the route he had taken into the Republik.

The way out is the way in.

He would require a little more cleverness than that.

Knowledge was not enough now. Wisdom was not to be hoped for.

· 109 ·

He knew that he didnt even have to make eye contact, simply walk by the man at exactly the pace one uses on retracing one's steps out of a museum, whatever that was, walk anyway, past him and the big dark grey Assyrian beards, out past the Egyptians and the Greeks and the Romans, the headless and those without penises.

Outward. He was walking through space that was theirs and time that was before him, putting it behind him.

Circling back to the entrance looking for an exit. His aim was the place where he had started. His end was beginning, no, his beginning.

He knew the man was following him, and he knew where

154

he was going. There would be no one downstairs in the toilet off the street, except the bitter-looking veteran who sat beside the saucer for aluminum coins. If he went down there, the swart man would not be able to follow him for fear of looking suspicious. But he would have to go down there sometime soon afterward, to make sure he was the first one to follow him.

He stood on the pavement, watching the beat-up little automobiles on Unter den Linden, waiting to make sure that anyone who might happen to be down in the hole would have time to shake it and come back up the stairs.

The espionage game is so sordid, he thought.

Finally he went down the dank steps, dropped fifty DDR pfennigs and fifty heavy western marks onto the saucer, might as well make a cold-war remark, but the bitter veteran was asleep with his eyes open, reliving the unhappiness of a supply clerk behind the Eastern Front.

While he was down there, what the hell, he took a leak. Then he went into one of the stalls no one should be obliged to describe, and lowered his trousers. The money took up a lot of space while it was distributed around one's funda-ment, and it made a very thick wad when one gathered it together. He took the string out of his shoulder bag and tied the bills into two bricks. Then he put them in the toilet bowl.

On the way out he washed his hands in cold water with ungiving brown soap, and tried to dry them on the pink towel hanging from a hook. He nodded alinguistically at the attendant, but the latter was still in the frozen Ukraine.

The swart man met him in the bright grey light at the top of the steps. He could not do anything now because the money might still be inside the blue Stanfield briefs. As he passed him and stepped down into the dark, he said, as if saying pardon me:

– Listen for the name of a city.

That did not make any sense, because this escapade was

over, would be over as soon as he got to the first West Berlin S-Bahnhof, would for certain be over the minute he got off the Lufthansa jet in Vancouver.

He crossed the street and walked down Unter den Linden toward Friedrichstrasse, pretty fast, toward brightness. In front of the fancy tourist hotel he stopped and looked back, casually. He saw the swart man step into the grey light out of the hole. The man hitched up his trousers, as anyone might do on coming out of a toilet, then walked away toward Alexanderplatz, eastward.

So it was really the end. But what, that familiar phrase, the name of a city. It sounded like another beginning.

· 110 ·

There should have been suspenseful music, plucked strings, runs of an electronic keyboard, then there should have been louder music, perhaps, as he walked briskly to the S-Bahnhof, horns, drums.

Afterward there might have been mellow music; he would, had he been asked, have thought of a sweet harp, a languid flute. Oh, how stupid, even the adjectives we lay on our brave clichés.

But there was no music. After the little rain shower the larks sang in the trees outside his apartment. And the subway train rumbled by.

In spy movies there was always something happening, all right, and plenty of dialogue, and something about to happen. Slowly things were learned, and then at last quickly.

He would settle for what he had learned, that little. He was looking forward to a day on which nothing would happen. He had had plenty of those in recent months, but he did not mind looking forward to at least one more. Then a plane flight over the pole, please, not the Poles, and often nothing happens during those, and that would be just fine.

He would listen for the name of a city, all right, but he wanted that name to be Vancouver, please, and he wanted to hear it over an airport public address speaker. Get home.

The Vancouver he would go to would not be the Vancouver he had left. He would not be the same person he was sure people referred to as Harry the Hack. He would still pursue his pride in handling the wheel right, and he would still spend his spare time devoted to his davenport and his television set. But none of those attractive places would be the places he had left in February. He would probably, he could now say, see a February again, and a June again, but not those he had stepped out of and into. The stream he was standing in now was not the one he had walked into in February, not by a long shot. Bad word. In February he did not know what fish swam by him. Now he had a taste for Pacific salmon.

He had acquired quite a lot of knowledge despite his daily puzzlement, and part of it was of himself, was himself.

· 111 ·

He was sitting at a corner table in the back room of the Thai Restaurant on Kaiser-Friedrichstrasse with Annalise, who said that the blazing food would be her treat.

The soup was not the classic shrimp and chili and lemongrass and lime leaf and peanut and garlic and cilantro and fish sauce soup, but it was something like it, and it was punishingly hot, so now, surrounded by deep red wallpaper and with the cylindrical bottle of an unfamiliar beer in his hand, he felt truly relaxed and ready for pleasant talk with the beautiful tall German woman, or silence, if that was what she wanted now.

The shrimp were tiny instead of the usual big tough ones opened like ribcages. The beer was dark and a little sweet, and it did nothing to alleviate the burning on the roof of his mouth and the sides of his throat.

−So, he said, I never knew that I would have to go through so much trouble to find a Thai restaurant and a lovely though spicily dangerous date.

− Was it worth it?

− Which?

− Oh you saucy Yank, she said.

− Dont start that.

She winced before another spoonful of soup.

− Well, you did get here, and that is what matters, isnt it?

He only grinned and kissed the air between them.

−I mean, she said, do you remember your mother making you hold your hands out, with a loop of wool around your wrists? While she pulled it toward her and wound it into a ball?

−I had forgotten all about that, he said. But it was my grandmother.

−Round and round, she said. Do you know why she wrapped it round and round?

−Tell me, he said, lighting a West cigarette from the candle because the waiter was not in sight.

− To keep it in a straight line, she said.

−All right. As you know more answers than anyone I have ever met, tell me this. Why was that woman in the coffin in Sydney dead? And who, while you are at it, was she?

−The reason why she was dead is simple. Some person thought that she was being contacted by a messenger. The same person thought that you were the messenger.

The waiter brought the dishes filled with hot brown food.

− Wonderful, he said.

− I have never eaten it before, she replied.

−No, wonderful. I could have been lying in a box in Sydney instead of on the sand at Henley Beach. What was her name? What was she following me from city to city for?

− Her name was Miss Krug. That is all ye need to know.

They ate for a while then, he with little exclamations of delight, she speculatively, looking carefully at each morsel.

– Well, he said, I am grateful to you for buying me a long-anticipated meal. I am thankful to be alive. And I am glad that this whole international literary and athletic fooforaw is over.

– Voovorahj?

– *Torheit.*

– But I must tell you that it is not quite over.

– Oh yes it is. For me it is. I am not going to walk around with any more legal tender in my private parts.

– Do you remember hearing over the telephone that you might want to take one extra plane trip for your own reason?

She was not talking enigmatically, not in circles. Just straight across the candle.

– Where, he asked.

Because how not?

– To Bern, she said.

· 112 ·

– Well, better to Bern than to marry, he told her after they had put up their feet and consumed a little of his good cognac in the sitting room of his apartment.

The management had turned off the heat according to the date, so it was not warm there on the first official night of summer. They therefore sat side against side on his couch, their feet on the magazines on his coffee table.

– You do not approve of the habit of marriage?

She was not quite as sexual as usual tonight. She was not leaning her bushy blond hair against him. She did not have a hand on his leg.

Some armoured personnel carriers rumbled by on Clayallee, getting ready for tomorrow's big military parade through the Tiergarten toward downtown East Berlin, more Yankee noise in the night, more war clatter in the middle of

159

the city whose people were more peaceable than any in the world now.

– Fire cools and is converted into earth and sea, he said.

– Those are nice elements too, she suggested.

Now she was not speaking for her own ardour. She was speaking for her own sex, inherited or chosen.

– How can I marry a person who was once the fastest man in the world, he asked.

And his voice betrayed his real hankering for an answer.

– Did you think of a fast man in that swimming pool in Perth?

He wanted to touch something, and he did. He put his fingers into her thick crisp hair, but he did it the way a person touches anything out of fondness.

– It's just that I keep thinking of her, as him at that moment, on the operating table. I keep thinking of parts, lying wherever the doctors put them.

– You can do that with anyone, she said. Think of my two hundred and some odd bones. You say some odd bones? They are all separate, a collection, no? But do you think of me that way?

– No, he said, smiling into his brandy glass, or rather his kitchen glass with brandy in it. I know what those bones can do when they act together.

– And I think about the way you men are, how you walk down a street, your eyes are isolating, yes? Bums and legs and bwests.

– Hair, he said. I look for hair across the street while I'm waiting for a light. I look for hair like yours.

– Thank you, I suppose, she said. I know how you feel about my hair. You have tried to put every separate piece of your body into it. But listen. I know you like my hair and other parts of me, but I know you love your Olympian, yes?

– If you insist, he said, yes.

– And you do not think of her, her, in pieces. You think of her all at once.

– I think of you all at once, he said.

– You may know a lot of particulars, she said, but it is a oneness you love. Is that right, oneness? That oneness is made from a great many particulars she has, not those she does not have. You should not put aside the idea of marrying if it comes up.

– I have to think about it, he said.

– When will you go to Bern?

– In a few days. I will give myself a few days to argue with myself. Myselves. Myselves are at war with one another.

– That is true concord, she said.

– Will you stay with me tonight while I begin to decide? As a friend?

– As a friend, she said.

· 113 ·

All over the world, all over television and the newspapers and magazines, airliners were being hijacked and blown up, falling from the sky into the sea, burning on runways, flying desperately from east to west and back across the Mediterranean.

Bombs were exploding in European airports and Asian luggage ramps. Every morning the radio woke him up with words about killed or imprisoned air passengers.

For the past four months he had been an air passenger too often.

Falling from the sky, scattered on the sea, burning on the ground, but always rising into the sky. He was surrounded like the globe with plot and incident. It was dotted with death and suffused with the great anxious desire for life.

He wished he could write. He was almost tired of reading. He was hungry for the aging transmogrified body of his dream in Switzerland. She had been his island of sanity in the Indian Ocean.

He was forty-nine years old, and still thought he was younger than the older ball players on the screen. But now he

161

was beginning to allow himself to think of himself as an old man. The young are amazed that they can become the old. The alive do not think of themselves as the dead. Yet nearly every night the awake all day become the asleep.

– Good morning, *Liebling*, said his friend.

He looked at the rain water edged with old chestnut blossoms on the concrete floor of the balcony, the terrace, they say here, or was that in Australia.

– Morning, anyway, he said. Another.

If it was morning, as it seemed to be, the asleep had become the awake. Surely, then, the dead would again become the alive, and most important, the old would re-emerge as the young.

For the globe this was allowable, this was true. But now it was more important that it should be true for him.

Abide with me, the best is yet to be.

– How old are you, he asked.

– Ah, remember that I am your friend.

In the death of fire is the life of water. Well, it was raining enough in this part of the world. Yet he heard a jet taking off from Schoenefeld airport just the other side of the wall.

· 114 ·

Sleeping.

Waking. The days were all the same, the same day, clouds like the bottoms of fish, in their element. And the nights were all one night. Here, it was said, people did not recognize night, but revelled on. Yet in his neighbourhood his was always the last light burning.

Abide with me, the rest is yet to be.

In Vancouver he liked to drive early in the morning, after the last drunks and before the first widowed shoppers. The drunks, and especially the Indian drunks, were the best

162

fares, the longest riders and the biggest tippers; but, fatal idiosyncracy in a cabbie, he liked to be alone sometimes, and there was no finer time to be alone than five-thirty in the morning, especially on the West Coast, when the exhaust fumes have given way to the old smell of the sea, where fish belong.

In his first year of driving, when he was nineteen years old, pretending to be twenty-two, a thickset man in a herringbone overcoat over a brown corduroy suit had got into his cab with some difficulty at five-thirty in the morning. He was about forty-five years old, spoke with a bluff English accent, and asked to be taken across the bridge.

– It will cost you, he had said.

– *No se puede vivir sin amar,* the man said.

He said it half a dozen times as the cab turned right off the bridge and drove in no traffic up the inlet.

He usually didnt talk to these guys because if he did get stiffed for the fare he did not want to have been cheated out of words too. But this one had an overcoat that would have fitted him, so he said that it looked like it would be the kind of morning or day one would not want to miss.

The man in the back seat made English grunts in his throat, and then (he usually forgot within a half-hour what his customers had said) started a long speech. He said that some Greek, our first Greek, he said, had got us off on the wrong foot by telling us that the day was the end of the night and *vice versa.*

– What is it, then, he asked.

– It is all night, the Englishman said, all one long night.

It made sense, somehow. The man lived in a shack, he said, but he had to let him off in the middle of the trees, next to a sad-looking path that went down through the willows.

But it turned out that he did have nearly enough for the full fare. There would have been enough if some of it hadnt been in Mexican money.

Well, close enough, he decided, and as he drove back he could see the sun bright on the top half of the Marine building, the bottom half in the darkness of sleep. Looking the other direction, he saw the blaze in the low air beside Mount Baker.

· 115 ·

He decided in favour of Bern because he felt as if he could not live without love, or maybe what he meant was that he did not want to go home without his sanity.

This is somebody who cares for you, Hairy. Well, that voice had said that all this was not really happening, that he was flying from country to country (that was happening, all right), making it all up. Maybe, though, the voice on the telephone was not happening, maybe he had made that up.

So he was going to the land of William Tell, and surely most people believed that they made that story up. They had invented a country of four languages, after all, where most people also manage English. An apple on a head. William Tell was real to them, a proper hero for an invented country with no walls except those the earth itself had thrust up.

I shot a jet plane into the air. It fell to earth I know not where. He was packed and ready to go to the Tegel airport, expecting and hoping for advanced German security, as telephone threats were delivered to air carriers all over the globe, and sharks swam between the Asian bodies in the Irish ocean.

William Tell invented a country with his shaft through the enraptured heart of the apple, eros on a mountain. It is not possible to make an invented country live without love, and now we know and sometimes chide Switzerland for its sanity, a country in which it is against the law to make noise at night.

The name of Tell's bow is *bogen* rather than *schliefe*, but its abandonment is life, a new life, a fruit riven and a mountain scatter brought together.

He would remove two letters from Berlin, the beginning of someone's name or of the second half of it, a Helvetian number fifty-one, the two added to his age, and he would have Bern. He wanted to see whether Bern would have him.

So his jumpy mind went, filled with too many particulars and too much caffeine. He would see whether Bern were the death or the life of fire. And who could tell.

8 · All Systems Go

· 116 ·

Bogen, Hell!

While he sat in the train for eight minutes at the station in Zurich, he looked out the window instead of reading the bad airplane news in the *Time* magazine on his lap. While he sat looking he saw a Swiss, presumably, in civilian clothes of a rustic cut and carrying a naked rifle. Then more and more men of nearly all ages carrying diverse rifles, and finally the youngest man of all carrying an ancient tassled and gold-threaded banner. They were all coming aboard the train, first this car, then after some argument the next one. That was a relief.

But how trusting in the goodness of man these Swiss people must be! For a person just come from the Berlin Wall, reading about public shootings and bombings all the way, it was a disconcerting little adventure.

So much so that he broke his rule and asked a Swiss about it. He was reminded of something he had been told about these peculiar people years ago, that the voting male citizens of this country that had not been at war in seven hundred years were obliged by their state to go out to the range and perform their target shooting from time to time.

– Do they still shoot apples off each other's heads, he asked.

But the man had heard that one before. And all the others.

After the drab flatness of postwar Berlin, Bern was very *glockenspiel*, very cuckoo clock. He loved the conscious arcades that lined the streets in the old city, and stepping beneath one, found himself a room at the Adler Hotel, *an der Gerechtigkeitsgasse.*

A quick expensive meal at No. 51, and then he went to his room, smoked three cigarettes, and went to bed. In the morning he would go for a walk under the fishy clouds, from one painted fountain statue to the next, hoping to find her on the street. They had given him an address, but he would not use it the first day. He was tired of messages on pieces of paper. He wanted to spot that head with the slightly greying hair unsuccessfully pulled back, bent, perhaps, at the window of a literary bookstore. He wanted to rely on the hidden harmony.

Certainly not a track-shoe store. Certainly.

· 117 ·

But the next day was blue and bright and altitudinous.

From the toilet he saw European summer at last, blue in the sky, and clothes drying on lines right outside his window.

He knew in his breastbone that the skies of central Europe were going to go on being a battleground, a game table, that the blue would push away the piled clouds, only to see the clouds return, flexing their power over ten countries. It was the long-range condition of the climate, the contention that made the trees grow and the trucks collide on the autobahn.

Yes, he was nervous.

It was the visible field of the hidden harmony, right up there, above, where airplanes were even now striving to remain afloat.

Except along or across the death strip through Berlin, the opposing forces make agreement, hold the universe together

– though taking part in the push of will and strength, people do not notice. They are kept in the dark and therefore the light, their ignorance the survival of themselves and them all. Perhaps along the death strip as well, where uneaten bunnies thrive.

He was experiencing this mock-profound line of thought while walking up the *Gerechtigkeitsgasse,* stopping with more indulgence than was his habit to examine the gaudy thematic statues at each fountain. The half-cooked musings of recent draftees in the spy occupation. Justice was brightly painted in yellow and green, and wore a white rag around her eyes. It fitted without bulk, like Shantung silk, perhaps.

Those thoughts continued their lopsided progress through his head, like a *glockenspiel* inside a glass bell inside rhyming gelatine, no colour at all unless the red-brown of dried blood.

He felt singularly sad when he thought how funny it was that they would have to to meet the day's sun in a country where it is against the law to make a noise at night. Maybe they had to pass that law because people here speak so loudly all the time.

It was, though, not what he had expected.

What did he expect now? He did not expect to see her on the street in Bern, not really, not within the first hour of his day.

There was also the question of what she expected. Whatever it was, he had no time to think about it. She had stepped up behind him and spoken very quietly in the contrail of his now unregardable thoughts.

· 118 ·

When they were together alone at last they did everything gradually.

Only gradually were they able to approach one another and kiss, and he remained on her lips only a moment,

169

moving his mouth to her neck then, and then closing his wet eyes against her untied hair shot with grey.

She leaned against him just a little, but it was a substantial little. He had wondered what her scent was, and had looked forward to remembering it, but it seemed at first that she had no scent, and then there was a little, not perfume but herself, a fine northern herb, close to the ground.

They solved the problem of not being able to speak for the nervousness of knowledge and distance and narrative, by not speaking at all, until they allowed short quiet sounds devoid of reference.

Let me follow you around the world, he had said in February, and now here at the end of June in Switzerland he followed her and she took him to where he wanted to go, a place he thought would be strange now that he knew some of the story, but it was a wordless place, not home, but against all odds sanity, or rather now the re-enlivened memory of sanity, and in this present her body was not as noisy as it had been in Perth, but it was a quiet turmoil.

Finally, with the sunlight coming as well as it could through the porous blue curtains and reaching even to them, he spoke simply.

– I love you, he said.

– Ah, she said.

Looking away, and then directly into his eyes. She was one year younger than he.

– I want you to come with me, he said.

There was a silence during which he noticed that they were not touching anywhere.

– I dont know, she said.

He did not touch her while he said the next thing. He wanted it to sound important and not just persuasive.

– I know that we are one, he said, wishing that he could

find a better word. It is not just me saying that. It is every-thing.

– The logos, she murmured.

– What?

– Everything, I suppose. But, she said, I dont know.

– Ah dear, I would like the, something, he said.

– The what?

– The wisdom. No. The sanity.

Get home, she had said again.

No, I will not leave Europe without you, he had said.

– Well then, get home to Berlin, she said.

Turning her back while she pulled her silk sweater over her head. He watched the athlete's aging muscles move below the skin. He understood why she did not want him to look at her hanging breasts.

– Sanity, he said.

– I do not know anything about that, she said.

Her back was still to him, though she was fully clothed now.

– Surely once you did. At –

– For a few seconds, once in a while. Always mixed with pain.

– And justification, he ventured.

– That was for God, she said.

And now she turned toward him. But the bed was between them. A streetcar could be heard descending the cobbled street at the front of the building.

– How can you say God, he asked.

He asked it quietly, but with a hope of encouraging, a hope that it would sound like a challenge from the endeared.

– You had to be a communist, he said, a member.

– Oh, God is a figure, she said. I mean of speech. Those few

171

seconds were like the wisdom you talk about so quaintly. No, not quaintly. It is more like loveable naivete. What one hopes to find in a Yank.

– Not –

– Like wisdom, those few seconds of at last doing it better, faster, farther really, than anyone thought one could. Then … are you listening?

He loved her utterly now, further down the tunnel than he had ever thought utter could be. He must have had a far distant look to his eyes.

– Yes, please, he said.

– I do not know why I should talk of this, she said. I left it behind me before it could leave me behind. It took years to do this, you wont ever know.

– Yes, but –

– Shut up. That wisdom, God it is, when you go right to the end as far as your body and your mind, yes, will be carried by your praxis. We call it God, but it is everything there at once. It is all one, and you go as hard as you can to be part of its one, and for a few seconds, well –

– You did it, he said. I love you like that. I would.

– God, she said.

And it would have been impossible for her to look at him now, as if he were a mere surgeon. But she spoke.

It allows you to call it God, but what is that? A word people use for their fear, for their nasty little single purposes. Both sides of the border. Yet they are themselves only little bits of dust in the river.

– River?

– A stupid word, she said.

– Will you come to Berlin?

– You will go, she said. I will come in a day or two days, no more than that.

– Ah, he said.

– Or I will not come. I will telephone.

– Again?

– I have never telephoned you before, she said.

· 120 ·

Back in Berlin, alone as one can be under the eyes of border guards and spies, he went where he was always drawn, to the ratty little corner off Potsdamstrasse, where ugly souvenir stands crowded around the foot of an observation platform upon which stood bus tourists pointing their cheap cameras over the wall at the death strip and the squat grey buildings on the other side.

He kept looking over his shoulder for the absent females, the women. As far as he could see, they were not there. They had not been there on the Yankee airliner that had brought him, disconsolate over the execrable Pan Am snack, through the drab corridor to West, heaven help us, Berlin.

He felt abandoned in the middle of the continent.

Grown Yankee men were walking around the squalid scene, pushing sticks of ice cream into their mouth holes. Some teenage girls giggled while they ran their ring-clustered fingers over the tawdry stuffed bears and key-chains, mementos of the cold war. They seemed to consider the wall just another wall.

There was a thin man in paint-daubed overalls covering all the old graffiti on the concrete with the usual contemporary mural, bright colours laid in curved lines next to other bright colours, so that now the popular culture of the west might be codified in its baseness rather than simply a scattering of individual and international reportings of clichés.

He had been looking these five months or almost for wisdom, and now here he was, almost bereft of thought, stunned by the unremitting grungy weather of east central Europe. The rain began as a mist and soon became a veritable torrent, and he did not care. He walked away from the wet

173

wall, through mud and past old dog shit and ice-cream wrappers, toward the west, his hair plastered to his head.

He understood why the poems of Charles Bukowski were popular in Germany.

Yet he felt as though she would telephone and say yes of course, or she would, better than that, be wet and huddled in his doorway when he got back to his apartment.

People who seek wisdom should make themselves familiar with a great many particulars. He had, or someone had, told himself that in eastern Australia.

There was a louder than ever roar in the sky. Looking up, he saw a huge dark triangle with an inquisitive beak, moving without gestures toward the eastern half of the city. It was the Concorde. He saw the British insignia on the tail.

It was June 30. The only other time he had seen the thundering Concorde had been that other dark grey day in Sydney, February 14. Human ingenuity had concurred to make such things possible. One had to understand the matter of opposition and cooperation. The local is understandable to all people, or none would be here. With a secret or without. The awesome aircraft must be a sign.

He was boring himself. The rain fell like a river he had stepped into once and could not now find his way to step out of.

The Concorde was gone into the grey, presumably to bank its huge solid metal triangle and descend back across the wall. Wisdom, he heard, without caring, is one and whole – it is to understand the knowledge, of which, after all this intelligence work he felt he had none to speak, by which all things are guided in their flightpaths by all other things.

Oh, sure.

Well, he thought, the story is over, and who was writing it?

Who was the writer. Of course she was back in London, talking with her long-time publisher, planning, perhaps, a best-seller out of all this, or at least part of it. If she had any brain left. If they had not washed her brain away in an apartment on Leipzigerstrasse, or more probably at some laboratory residence in a university town.

In any case, he remembered, consciousness is how it is composed.

But it extends deep beyond comprehension in every direction, a voice said. It was the voice of a drunk he had met thousands of kilometres away, and he was not there. No one was there.

And nothing, he knew, was there, out there.

So he was here, in a messy little Greek bar in West Berlin, waiting for fate or her decision, or fate. Waiting for the logos.

The reason he was thinking such ponderous and fruitless thoughts in neither of the languages he heard thudding around him was that he had had an unremembered number of lovely bulbous glasses of German beer that appeared in front of him with thick brown foam on top, and once, out of lonely bravado described silently to himself as simpatico, an oily glass of ouzo.

Though as a taxi driver he favoured narrative over meditation because it was more likely to be accompanied by monetary income, and though in Vancouver he appreciated a rainy day because borderline pedestrians are more likely to decide on a cab when it is wet, he was stuck here, engaged in meditative, perhaps, thoughts, justified in his endurance because it had been raining out there on Kaiser-Friedrichstrasse and probably the rest of the city all afternoon and all evening.

And here is one thing he wound up thinking. Some people use the word God, or in a restaurant such as this, Zeus, to refer to the entirety of fate or design or a streetmap called otherwise the logos. God is a name for day and a name for night. Also a name for satisfaction and a name for want.

When we run out of names we get to the actual thing, but we never run out of names.

Maybe we never run out of want.

· 122 ·

Midweek he woke, and sat up to the sun.

He rushed to see the sky that was blue from side to side. The fire in the sky was there the same every day, high, but now the clouds were not low, and today if he went any-where, he would saunter out, yes, saunter, and he would not carry his umbrella, he would be, relatively, free. He had dreamt of a magazine, but nothing in it.

The sun was here instead of there. There was some justice in the world after all.

Actually, more than he could wish. It was not there when he first sat up, but now it was here, a Greek hangover. He wished it were made up, part of a mere narrative. He would erase it or scratch it out. Or he would ask her to.

The sky was high and he heard a jet plane pass over. What a great day for flying. Say from Switzerland to West Berlin, or West Berlin to Zurich.

The sun lay along the top of the concrete wall of his terrace this *Mittwoch* morning, turning it white. It was white as her skin inside her grip, her inside thigh. In most women her age an inside thigh would be wide and loose, but she had been an athlete. His eye went from her thigh.

If there is any justice in the world she will come, he thought. If the sun can come after all these months of rain, then so can she, after all these months.

Otherwise, what did I cross the line for? The line and the other line and then especially the other line.

Once in a while we need the coming of justice to keep things in line. Otherwise the sun might stray, and she or I might stay away.

Even with a Greek hangover it would be a nice day.

· 123 ·

Yes, it was summer, so now the sun was already there when he woke the next day.

Everything will come when its season says so.

So he spent all day beside the telephone. Well, that is what they say. He spent all day in his apartment, while the sun traversed the upturned bowl of the sky, its sky. It rose out of East Berlin, which was strange, and sailed over the wall as easily as a blazing bird or a blaring *blas-orchester*. Then it headed toward western Europe and perhaps the Americas.

Then the air outside his apartment grew dark, but as it grew dark it grew noisy, because this was the fourth of July, and drunken U.S. military people and their children were passing by, yelping and hooting, smashing overhead lights, carrying portable tape-players with execrable Yankee or Southern music played as loud as it would twist.

The squat green telephone with the white swirls in the plastic, however, was silent as a forgotten battlefield.

Everything, he told himself, drinking a little *Jagermeister* out of the trim glass that had once held mustard, will come when its season says so. It should.

· 124 ·

Finally the telephone did ring.

It rang with, perhaps, a tone of finality. He had been sleeping in one of the soft chairs, all through the second half of the night.

He stumbled to the telephone and lifted the hand unit, dropped it on the other part, and lifted it again to his face.

– Good morning, he said.

177

Then he looked to the window and saw sunlight along the edge of the terrace.

It was she.

– Were you asleep, she asked.

– I was sleeping, he said, by the telephone.

I dont sound as intelligent as I could wish, he thought.

– Even sleepers are cooperating in the work of the universe, she said.

And laughed lightly, or almost.

– Here you are at last, he said.

– You mean here on the telephone, I presume, she said. Really I am here in Bern, you should know.

He did not want to ask the decisive question. If it would go as he thought it would go, he would rather receive it as an extension of his sleep, passively, so that it would not seem that he had collaborated in the bringing of the news. His thoughts told him that he was still half asleep. The nature of his thoughts told him so.

– I suppose, she said, that you know what I am going to tell you.

– Yes, he said.

He was in fragments around the globe.

She spoke after the shortest of pauses.

– I regret it, she said.

Then he was awake.

– Damn it, he said. All this, all this, whatever it was. It was supposed to have a meaning. A meaning at last.

– It has been a part of everything else, she said.

Her voice was calm, like the voice of an analyst, or a parent.

– I love you, he said. That is one thing I did find out. When I am with you, when I was with you, I have never known anything else like that.

There was another very slight pause.

– It is possible to live without love, she said. *Se puede vivir.*

– But what is more important than that, he asked. You are my sanity. What is more important than that?

– It is possible to live without love, she said. But permission is necessary.

The sky of West Berlin was blue as far as the birds could see.

– Seeing, then, he said. Do you think I will see you again?

– Here in Switzerland there are people who make a great thing out of coincidence, though they call it something else. You have told me that your life in recent months has seemed full of coincidences. We should perhaps say synchronicity, *ja?*

So much perhaps.

– Yes, but there wasnt any. It was all the questionable planning of the editorial board, and your former socio-political organization, and, I suppose, certain western clinics, and now I suppose they were or are in Switzerland. Are the mountains beautiful this morning?

– Yes, they are.

– How are you going to live, he asked.

His voice working to contain disappointment and a certain resolution.

– Oh –

– What will I do now?

– Get home.

– What will you do? How will you live now?

– I can live a modest life on my royalties. Goodbye, you nice man.

– What?

But the telephone in his hand was only some unattractive green plastic without intelligence.

What.

– Sydney, Feb 14, 1985
– West Berlin, July 5, 1985

Editor for the Press: Frank Davey
Cover Design: Paul Sych / Reactor
Cover Photo: Floria Sigismondi
Text Design: Nelson Adams
Typeset in Palatino and printed in Canada

For a list of other books
write for our catalogue

Coach House Press
401 (rear) Huron Street
Toronto, Canada M5S 2G5